## *NEW YORK TIMES* BESTSELLING AUTHOR
# EVE LANGLAIS

# DRAGON MISFIT

Copyright © 2020/2021 Eve Langlais

Cover Art © 2020/2021 Dreams2Media

Produced in Canada

Published by Eve Langlais

http://www.EveLanglais.com

eBook ISBN: 978 177384 1885

Print ISBN: 978 177384 1892

This book is a work of fiction and the characters, events and dialogue found within the story are of the author's imagination and are not to be construed as real. Any resemblance to actual events or persons, either living or deceased, is completely coincidental.

No part of this book may be reproduced or shared in any form or by any means, electronic or mechanical, including but not limited to digital copying, file sharing, audio recording, email and printing without permission in writing from the author.

**PROLOGUE**

2:36 P.M., *July 14$^{th}$*
*Beep. Beep.*
The machines steadily recorded the fact that Subject Z showed no sign of life other than slow, deep breathing and the thumping of his two hearts.

An oddity that puzzled the doctors. Why two? If they could have, they would have dissected him, split open his body, delved around inside. However, given he was one of a kind, they were loath to lose him. The original scientists put a lot of effort and money into creating Z and then thought they'd lost him during an unfortunate mishap that saw him escaped. Now that Chymera Tech Industries had caught him again, they wanted to get their money's worth.

A good thing CTI already had an installation that could not only contain him but also provided blood testing on the main floor. They'd had steady business since the pandemic freak-out. People and governments became more paranoid and vigilant. Most of the labs used unknowing techs handling the bloodwork as a façade to hide the true heart of Chymera below.

The state-of-the-art medical facility provided a range of services from genetics to measurements of strength, endurance, and durability. There was an entire level dedicated to housing the subjects. Massive operating rooms that could accommodate even the most ferocious, like Z. A good thing they had several layers of security. An equipment malfunction led to him waking. A lot of good people died before he was sedated.

In case it happened again, they increased the number of guards nearby and armed them with enough narcotics to take out a herd of elephants. They'd thought of every possibility and put in measures to stop it.

And then the lights flickered. Screens stuttered. Machines beeped in warning. Technicians all over the building paused in their tasks. The light steadied.

People heaved a sigh of relief. Too soon, as it turned out.

It went dark. Suddenly. The quiet proved heavy as the hum of electricity disappeared. The dark wrapped the room. No exterior windows, not even a hint of light. In that cloying space, someone panicked.

"Holy fuck. It's dark. I don't like it. Someone turn on the lights. Shit. I need a flashlight."

He kept going on and on until someone else said, "Shut up, Simon."

Simon shut up.

A good thing because hysteria was contagious.

"Anyone got a flashlight?"

Phones, that was what they had. The screens lit up the space, making it eerie, but familiar too.

It was Veronica who suddenly reminded them of the larger problem at hand. "Um, how long can Subject Z go without drugs before he wakes up?"

"Not long."

"Oh fuck."

"We need to get out."

Voices from all over spoke at once, even as they surged for the elevator, their cellphones leading the way. They'd forgotten two key things.

One, the elevators wouldn't work without electricity, and two, they were locked in until the power came back. A safety feature to keep the danger contained within.

Veronica stood at the interior viewing window, aiming her phone down into the room where Z slept.

"Can you see him?" Hailey—who sometimes brought in dry gluten-free and sugar-free peanut butter cookies—asked. She also shone her phone down.

"I think I saw Z moving," Veronica stated.

"Did you?" Hailey asked. "Because I can't see him. It's too dark."

The sudden hum drew a scream from someone,

only to turn into a nervous laugh as the lights returned. People blinked but also quickly ran to their stations, a few to the window to glance below.

Z twitched, and it goaded them to work faster. Fingers flew on keyboards as technicians scurried to reboot systems and restart machines. Every second felt longer as the precautions that tamed him remained offline. The IV wasn't enough. They had to disrupt other things and needed electricity to do it.

"Electromagnetic field coming back online," Simon shouted.

"Where is the EMP at?" shouted Gary, team leader of the week. They rotated so as to keep everyone on their toes.

"Still charging up," Klive announced.

But it didn't appear as if they'd need it. Z remained stretched and manacled. Eyes closed, breathing slow, even, unchanged.

Crisis averted.

It was Kiara, in charge of monitoring his brain activity, who stated softly and somewhat nervously, "I have a blip."

A blip? It was so unexpected that many crowded around and glanced at her screen.

Blip.

They all saw the slight jump in the brain wave pattern. Considering the usual flat line, it provoked consternation and questions.

"Simon, are you sure the field is up and full power?" Gary barked.

Simon peered at his screen as if his nose pressed to it would change what he saw. "Unless we've got some bad sensors, then it's not my stuff."

"Someone needs to check his IV. Make sure it's still flowing," Gary demanded.

"On it," Bethany said as she headed for the door. She'd have to go down a level to manually inspect the drug vat.

Hours of checking, with the boss coming in and breathing down their necks, and they couldn't find anything wrong. And Z's brain kept blipping.

"What does it mean?" someone asked.

"Is he awake?" was the next query.

"Better hope not."

Because Z would kill, and he didn't need to touch them to do it.

## CHAPTER 1

DEAR DIARY: TODAY IS MY BIRTHDAY.
THIRTY-THREE YEARS SINCE I HATCHED.

My parents knew the day I cracked out of my egg that there was something different about me. Not entirely surprising, given they'd stolen said egg from a government lab as part of some free-the-animals-from-cruel-testing movement. Apparently, my parents and some other liberal thinkers of the time stormed a research facility known for using animals.

Back in those days, security wasn't as thorough as today and the locks were easier to break. The liberation group marched en mass into the facility, sweeping past the guard on duty and making it into the inner bowels, where they opened up cages, letting the animals out. Which, as it turned out, wasn't exactly good for the neighborhood. Rats, especially smart lab ones, proved to be a nuisance. And the monkeys? There were reports to this day that hikers in the adjacent woods still spotted them, usually a second before poop was flung at their heads.

Add in a few pigs, some cats, several dogs, and even—or so my mom claimed—a horse, and it created quite a menagerie of escaping animals. With freedom at hand, those animals ran. But what of the eggs the protestors discovered being kept warm inside a lab?

It seemed wasteful to smash them. My mom said my jewel-like shiny purple shell called to her. Never mind the fact it took two hands to carry the egg, she smuggled it home with the help of my dad.

Once there, she placed the egg—with me inside—on their mantel above the fireplace. Given my mom always complained of a chill, the gas fireplace ran almost continuously. Anyone with basic science knowledge knows heat rises, and while not an incubator, it kept my egg toasty warm.

It was during the holidays, as my parents enjoyed a marathon of *Die Hard* movies, that I was born.

Kind of.

I cracked my egg.

Being the type who photographed everything, my parents took pictures of my birth and even managed a short video too—still on a VHS tape buried in my memory box under my bed. Every so often I pulled it out and played it.

It was funny to listen to my mom and dad as they wondered what would come out of the giant egg.

*Dad: Maybe we should take it outside in case it's smelly and messy.*

*Mom: It's much too cold.*

*Dad: What if it's dangerous?*

*Mom (uttering a snort): Pretty sure we can handle a baby bird.*

*Dad: That bird is bigger than your head.*

*Mom: More to love.*

*Dad: And if it's a gator with teeth?*

*Mom: Reptiles need love, too.*

My mom never saw a stray she didn't adopt, whereas my dad grumbled about every extra mouth even as he carried around treats in his pockets. We fed all the neighborhood cats. We had bird feeders everywhere—which caused a dilemma since the cats considered those birds dinner, too.

I had a gamut of pets my entire life. Although since I'd moved out—against my mother's protests—I'd whittled down to only a single dog.

Watching my birth video, I was always in awe and breathless as I saw the first crack, the one that got things started. It was just a hairline thing that spread, crackling the shell, splintering it. Instinct must have driven me because I don't remember being inside trying to get out. I will say that my welcome to the world versus the one I saw in sex ed later on in high school made me happy I'd come out a less traditional way. There was a lot less blood and screaming.

My mom could be seen off to the side, bouncing and squeaking. She was so excited, wondering if I'd have plumage. Dad kept telling her to step back in case there were claws instead of feathers.

They both stopped talking when, in the video, you could see my fingers emerge, and then my clenched fist as I manage to shove a chunk of shell out of my way. Things remain quiet until my mom finally whispered, "What the fuck is that?"

A word I heard a lot growing up. My parents weren't the kind to hold back from expressing themselves in language that, when repeated, got me in trouble with other grownups.

"Is that a baby?" My dad sounded so baffled. I could just imagine him shoving his glasses up on his nose. Scratching his head. The adorable scholar slash activist.

You can hear my mom scoff. "It can't be. Babies aren't born in eggs."

"Technically they are," my dad corrected.

"Not those kinds of eggs," my mom argued. "Maybe it's a monkey."

There was a time in my youth that I pretended I was a monkey. A smart one like in *Planet of the Apes*, who could talk and do all the things humans do.

I wasn't a monkey. Anyone could see that the moment my head poked through the shell, my hair sticking up in dark streaks. My eyes blinked at the light. My mouth oh-ed in awe.

I was adorable. Like seriously, I had the pictures to prove it.

"It's not a monkey. Jumping Jehovah, it's a bloody human baby." Then my dad said, "Fuck!" about twenty times in a row. And that was when the video, ended but I know the rest of the story, a favorite of mine growing up because my parents never hid the truth from me.

As they told it, my mom ran for the mantel before I could fall off. She plucked me from the remnants of the shell and hugged me close.

She told me, *"You are a miracle. A gift from God."* A blessed surprise to a couple who couldn't conceive a child of their own and never even thought of giving up the baby born from an egg, even though she came with a tail.

## CHAPTER 2

DEAR DIARY: I HATE SKINNY JEANS. WHY COULDN'T PARACHUTE PANTS COME BACK IN STYLE?

I CAME into this world with a tail. Not a big one. Just a little wiggly nub at the end of my spine. Now, most people would have chosen to have it removed. Booked me in with the surgeon and sawed it right off.

My parents obviously weren't most people. For one, they realized immediately how special I was. And two, they were strongly of the opinion that decisions pertaining to my body belonged to me. What did that mean other than no chopping my tail? No earrings until I was old enough to make that decision on my own—and regretted for a few days given it hurt! Had I been a boy my dad said they wouldn't have circumcised me. I went through a few bouts of tonsillitis when I was young, but my parents refused to let them take those suckers out. Which, as it turned out, was a good thing because the doctors might have noticed I wasn't like other little girls.

I kept my tail, and my parents kept me. They registered my birth with the state, claiming they had me at home without a midwife. A good thing those handing out birth certificates never saw me with my parents because they might have questioned how a truly Caucasian couple—dad had red hair and mom was a sandy blonde—ended up with a very obviously Asian-featured child.

People who met us as a family unit assumed adoption. I always knew the truth, except for who my biological parents were. Given I was made in a lab, the original egg and sperm donors probably never even knew I existed. I assumed I got the tail from my mother, given the whole egg thing.

I knew I'd never know the truth. The lab I was stolen from had burned to the ground, along with its secrets.

I was thankful my parents saved me from a life I couldn't imagine but studied via science fiction films and comic books. I used fiction to find answers, because what else could a girl with a tail born from an egg do? It wasn't as if we could ask any doctors or run any tests.

From an early age, my parents taught me to keep my specialness a secret. They explained how people wouldn't understand. Might try to hurt me. Bully me. Take me into custody and do unspeakable things. The movies and books all agreed, which was why I was homeschooled for the early years and had few outside interactions with other kids.

But don't imagine for a second Mom and Dad kept

me locked up. I was allowed to go to the park. I played on a few sports teams. Not that I was very good at it. I even learned how to swim when my parents had a pool with a privacy screen installed, because while I could hide my tail under clothes, a bathing suit showed all.

Eventually, my mom relented when at eleven I begged for them to let me go to a real school. By then I was a pro at hiding my butt. Loose pants where I could tuck my tail down my leg. Baggy shirts. It wasn't easy at first. My socializing skills needed some work after I'd spent most of my time with my parents and other adults.

Over time, and with dodged perseverance—plus an addiction to dweeb-turned-popular-girl movies—I adjusted. I even went on to high school. Did the things teenage girls did. Smoked cigarettes. Tried weed. Made out under the bleachers. Had a boyfriend that didn't last long. The kissing part was great, but when he went to grab my butt...things went downhill.

Tears were shed as he called me a freak. My mom did her best to console me. Dad bought me ice cream. They told me to forget what Brandon said. Extolled my virtues.

I hid my pain inside and only spilled it in my mental diary—because I didn't dare write anything down. But I had to talk to something, so I kept one inside my head and spilled everything.

After the Brandon fiasco, and because of the nickname devil girl, I ended up finishing my senior year at home. With my grades, I easily got into college. When I graduated, I got a job, made some friends, and life was good, if a tad lonely.

In good news, I did eventually lose my virginity. In the bathroom of a club, where dim lights, a drunk guy, and a skirt that could be lifted meant he never saw a thing.

It wasn't the only time I resorted to that method. I was a woman in my prime craving love and attention. I didn't want to be alone forever, but how could I ever trust anyone with my secret?

How could I expose my parents to the possible repercussions? They'd warned me if it was discovered they'd stolen company property they'd be in trouble. They never listened to my counter argument. That lab made a lizard baby, totally illegal, and the proof? Exhibit A, my tail.

When I said I'd had enough and was going public, Mom cried that she'd go to jail. Dad looked disappointed in me. I promised to never ever tell anyone.

And then they went and died on me. At 5:37 p.m., on a sunny July 14$^{th}$, I found out my life was a lie. Everything they'd told me...

LIE.

Ten seconds later after my discovery, half of the East Coast had a power failure. It should be noted I planned to eat all the ice cream anyhow. The corner store down the street was more than happy to sell me theirs half price, and I ate that, too.

The power failure lasted days, and during that time, there was a mad rush to ensure the generators didn't fail. Guards were stationed around Subject Z's room. Someone watched him at all times with a hand by the emergency button that would lock down the facility.

The drug levels remained steady and even increased. His magnetic shields and the dampening systems all active. He couldn't be waking yet since the moment the lights went out, there'd been a steady blip.

Impossible.

Why was his status changing? What changed it?

No one knew. They could only watch and wait and hope it didn't kill them.

## CHAPTER 3

DEAR DIARY: MY PARENTS ARE ASSHOLES.
WHY DO I MISS THEM?

My parents left me a letter when they died. And reading it the second time, I remained just as enraged.

Finding out the truth—the real truth, not the pretty, wrapped-in-a-bow lie I'd been told my whole life—had me pissed. Thirty-three years I'd believed a load of bullshit. Been steered into not asking questions. Not daring to demand where I came from.

It had been part of a larger betrayal by the two people I'd trusted most.

How could they?

They were dead, and I couldn't ask, and I wanted answers, which was why I uprooted myself, moved from the only home I ever knew, taking only what would fit in my truck—which was a ton of stuff given I drove a big-ass, shiny black Suburban. A monster on gas. Seriously, if I so much as thought about my truck, it lost a quarter-tank. But I loved the beast. Massive in size, fully loaded. I went all out and had the payment each month to prove it. But who else did I have to spend my money on?

With my parents dead and me their sole heir, I actually managed to clear my debts and still have a nest egg big enough I could technically live off it for a few years. Could have but wouldn't. I preferred to work.

Given both my parents taught at a university—mathematics for Dad, chem for Mom—I gravitated toward science from a young age. I fucking loved science. Nothing better than immersing myself in a good thick textbook that delved deep into studies and provided testing results. Give me the numbers. Those yummy, yummy stats.

I couldn't get enough, which was why, before I graduated high school, I had an unofficial degree in molecular biology. Why not get the real thing?

My parents said it might draw attention. Me, the result of a science experiment working in science? It made sense at the time to my young, apparently dumb brain. I ended up training in college to be a lab technician. As a job, it allowed me some leeway when it came to testing myself.

While my parents had a don't-ask, just-hide mentality, as I got older, I couldn't help but be curious. Who was I? What was I?

Like seriously, what?

As I grew older, my tail grew with me, going from a stubby nub to knee-long whip by my twenties, then to my ankles before it started thickening and developed a spade tip. The shade of purple on the scales was the same hue as the egg that hatched me.

Now, you might wonder how hard it was to hide in public with a big honking tail. Easier than expected. People just assumed I had a giant ass because I wore long, baggy shirts and loose trousers. I kept my tail trapped to my leg, so it didn't flop around. If I wore a skirt down to my calves, I folded my tail and plastered the spade into the middle of my back with a special belt.

Not exactly comfortable, or ideal, and as I got older, with the tail getting even bigger, I worried people would start to notice. The other morning, I could have sworn I saw nubs bulging my forehead, making me wish I'd test driven some bangs during the last pandemic. Did I have a face for a short fringe? Should I try a side-part first?

More differences between me and non-eggies? I had a lot of teeth. At least six more than was normal, not that any dentist had a record of it. My parents took care of me. I only rarely went to see any doctors and that only because, as my mother explained, it would be weird if I went my entire life never seeing one. So I saw the eye doctor and a family doctor who gave me shots that pinched only a little and resulted in a lollipop. I liked the purple ones best.

The one doctor I'd never seen? A gynecologist. No way I could hide my tail from them, and at my age, I'd long ago decided I wasn't getting rid of it. The tail belonged to me. I couldn't just hack off a part of myself.

*But what am I? Where did I come from? And more important, are there others? More science experiments like me?*

It would be nice to know I wasn't alone.

The letter my parents left gave me the name of the company that had made me. Chymera Tech Industries. They had all kinds of satellite locations around the world, but what do you know, its headquarters was only two states over from me. And they were hiring.

I drove there in my packed Suburban, along with the box of lies inherited from my parents, not a tiny shoebox either. We're talking a full-sized business box. They'd kept it inside their closet, in a safe I never suspected existed. They left me the location and combination in their will, along with that damnable letter.

I should have burned it but, instead, read it over and over as if maybe the hundredth time it would make sense.

My truck drank the cheapest gas I could find as I drove. Guzzling it like a guy who'd given up on pacing his beer. It chugged, and I paid because if I wanted answers, real and true ones, I needed to go back to the beginning. The lab my parents took me from was where it all began, but it had burned down. That at least was true. I'd seen the newspaper clipping.

According to my research, Chymera Tech Industries—commonly referred to as CTI and using an emblem consisting of a lion with a spiked tail and wings usually in gold—rather than rebuild the lab they lost, added on to a different installation. My hope was I'd find records of the old lab inside the CTI building. To that purpose, I applied for a job opening they advertised for a lab tech. I had more than enough experience with blood samples. I could run sequences with my eyes closed. A job would give me access to the computers and the network, plus the entire building if I played my cards right. Years of stealthy testing on the side had led to me having a knack for being in places I shouldn't.

Even before CTI hired me, I hit the road with my dog by my side. Literally, he took over the passenger seat despite the dog bed I'd set up in the back.

Meet Murphy. Part everything. DNA testing showed he had seven different strains in him resulting in an oversized, long-haired, fluffy meathead. My dog was dumb. But cute. The only friend I had left in the world. He also slobbered all over my lap, so that when we arrived in front of our new digs—the second floor of a converted house—I emerged appearing as if I peed myself.

Great. Just fucking great, because, of course, the guy living on the first floor—attractive fellow, if you were into blonds—happened to be outside. He saw my wet crotch and, as expected, looked grossed out.

"It's not pee but dog slobber." Which in some respects might not have sounded any better.

Rather than reply, he went inside. Suited me fine. I'd rather not make really awkward conversation. With some people, it didn't matter how nice or intelligent I was. Some only judged by appearance, putting more emphasis on body shape and size. Assholes in other words.

Sound mean? Call it a pet peeve of mine. Dislike me because I'm a bitch or a twat. Don't do it because my bottom half appeared wide. Not my fault I was big-tailed.

I opened the passenger door, and Murphy joined me in the driveway. He was waist high and a leaner. I'd learned to brace myself when he swayed.

The second floor had a steep set of stairs leading upwards. A rail bolted to the house and another rail at the far edge of the steps. Murphy lumbered past me, wedging his big body, almost sending me tumbling. He didn't have a gentleman's bone at all in that shaggy body. At the top, the stairs widened into a small porch, big enough I might be able to manage a chair, maybe a plant. If I stayed here that long.

My dog waited for me to open the door, bored and impatient, late for his next nap. I leaned over him and tried to fit the key that the landlord had sent me via express post. New locks were the worst. Figuring out the quirks. Would it require pulling or pushing on the handle to make it tighter or looser for the lock to disengage. Would the key stick? How hard do you have to turn? What if I accidentally snapped the key?

*Click.* Still my dog didn't move, so I kept leaning on him to turn the handle and open the door. The moment it opened, my dog moved, and I almost fell flat on my face.

I caught myself and peeked quickly inside. Fitted into the angled eaves of the house, the apartment contained a cute kitchenette with an island and three stools instead of a kitchen set. The living room was right beside with a skylight above it. Through the open door across the way was a bedroom, the mattress on the box frame giving it away. I'd rented the place furnished. In my truck I had all I needed. Clothes. Murphy's bed. A few memories. And the box of lies.

It took me several trips up and down the stairs. Despite what people might think, given my bulky clothing and narrow top versus wide bottom, I wasn't out of shape. I carried massive armloads each time I skipped up and down those steps. I wasn't even breathing hard by the fourth trip down, and my neighbor, who'd exited his place, noticed.

"You must be in great shape to handle those stairs so well," stated McBlond, his hair the generic golden of a French fry.

I grabbed the fifty-kilo bag of dog food, good for maybe three days, and hefted it onto a shoulder. "I like being active." I might not always be coordinated about it, but I didn't lack stamina or strength.

"What regime do you follow? Because that's impressive." He actually sounded sincere.

"When I have time, I go to the gym to push weights, and I jog." A lie. But my parents told me I should never admit it just came naturally. I didn't have to exercise or diet.

"I'm Ben," McBlond said, holding out a hand.

I shook it with the one not holding the dog food in place. "Kalini." My mother told me she chose it because of its Greek meaning: pure. Hardly pure in my case, but it could have been worse. At least it was easy to spell.

"How long you staying for?" Ben asked.

A valid question given I'd rented the place from one of those online short-term rental apps. "Three months and then we'll see." My contract with CTI would be done by then and hopefully I'd have my answers.

"In town for pleasure?"

My first impulse was to say, *Have you looked around?* Which wouldn't set the right tone if he happened to love his town. I stuck to, "I got a job at a local lab. Chymera Tech Industries."

"No shit." Ben grinned. "I work there, too. We call it CTI for short."

I knew he worked there since I'd pulled up a roster of people publicly listed as company employees then further checked to see who had active addresses. It wasn't hard to find something near one of them. I'd lucked out and got an apartment right over their head of public relations.

"Wow, what a small world," I tittered, because it seemed like the right thing to do. "Guess we'll see each other a lot. At work," I reiterated in case he thought I was hitting on him.

"You know what, we should carpool."

When I'd decided to move in above Ben, I'd expected to have it take a few days, maybe even a week before he realized the new woman at work was his neighbor. I hadn't even unpacked my toothbrush and he was tossing himself at me. The man who probably had access to everything at CTI.

I didn't fool myself into thinking I could seduce him. McBlond wasn't the type to go for anything less than an eight. On my best day, I was probably a six, and only because I was cute. There was nothing special about me to make me stand out—long, straight black hair, a small mouth, dark eyes. I didn't break mirrors. I also didn't shatter any records.

"What do you say?" he prodded.

"We totally should." I could make that work to my advantage. Maybe get him to spill CTI's secrets, copy his keys, get close enough I could somehow infiltrate.

And then I saw it. His car. Not really a car. The parked toy could fit in the back of my truck.

He noticed me looking and beamed. "It is the most recent electric model on the market. The body is like one giant solar panel and battery in one."

"I could bench press it," I muttered. That wasn't a car.

"It's environmentally friendly."

Did this guy who worked for a lab known to do research that used animals for testing really want to claim he was eco-inclined?

"Doesn't look like there's room for a passenger," I remarked.

"Plenty of room. You'll see," he boasted with a smile so perfect I'd bet he'd had lots of work done.

"Or we could just drive together in my truck." When he opened his mouth, I hurried to shut it. "I'll pay for the gas."

"You will?"

"Yup. I prefer to be the one driving, and I'm more than happy to give you a ride. I was told the company has very strict working hours."

Ben nodded. "Literally eight to five, with one hour for lunch. By five after, the place is empty."

"What if you're working on something?" I asked, because most places didn't care if someone lingered a few extra to finish a test or paperwork. They were salaried. It didn't cost the company extra.

"Doesn't matter. At five, everything shuts down, which is why carpooling is an excellent idea. It can be a little crazy when a hundred people are trying to all leave at once."

"Why not implement a staggered start and finish system?"

"No one complains." He rolled his shoulders. "When do you start?"

"Tomorrow."

"Then we'll meet at your truck at seven thirty-five."

How had we gone from him making a face at my appearance to him neatly arranging to get a free chauffeur Monday to Friday?

"Sounds good," I muttered and headed up the stairs with my dog food. I was sure I felt someone staring, but when I looked back, I saw nothing. Ben must have gone inside, and I saw no one else around.

Still...I locked the door and, as the dog food thumped to the floor, heard the fridge stutter. Not another place with electricity problems. It seemed to happen a lot lately.

Not that my dog cared. He lay across my feet and wouldn't budge until I said, "You hungry?"

---

A GOOD THING he'd just finished eating, because when Ben's phone went off, he knew he'd be a while. They'd called him in after hours because Subject Z showed signs of waking despite increasing his current drug dosage.

Blips of brain activity kept cropping up. A stirring of his eyes under the lids. Even a restless shift of the body. Ben wasn't the only who held his breath when something like that happened. They were playing with something very dangerous, and since the bosses made it clear they wanted him alive, Ben's job was to make sure Z and the others didn't escape.

Why weren't the drugs working anymore? Ben had to get close to Subject Z that he might check on the restraints, glance over the equipment, and verify the safety measures remained in place and ready to activate.

For a body that hadn't moved in a long time, Z's muscles remained firm, although there was a pallor to the skin and a gauntness that delineated bone and muscle. Everything in the room appeared secure, but out of curiosity, Ben lifted Z's eyelid and shone a light. The pupil didn't react one bit. He let it close and then froze as Subject Z inhaled through his nose and kept sniffing.

He shivered as Subject Z held his breath then huffed it out on a growl.

Oh fuck.

Ben backed away. "Feed him more juice."

The control room would increase the dosage in increments, watching Subject Z's vitals. They'd sacrifice Ben before their precious project. It was what had happened to his predecessor.

Luckily, Subject Z settled down except for the occasional brain blip. Being overly cautious, Ben stayed the night at CTI. He didn't get to his real bed until dawn.

Seeing the big truck as he dragged his ass home,

Ben was reminded he wouldn't be carpooling with his new neighbor who had a nice face but not the greatest figure. What she did have in abundance? Stamina. He knew very fit people who couldn't have jogged up and down those stairs, especially carrying stuff, so many times.

Having worked with Subject Z, as well as Q, F, and H in the other wings, he was better equipped to notice. To wonder. Was she related to a mutant? The company had admitted to Ben they'd had some issues in the past. Lost some labs and the experiments within. The most shocking thing of all, though, was finding out missing hybrids only crowned the tip of the iceberg. Monsters already lived among them. Hid from the humans.

CTI made it their duty to find and study them. In Ben's opinion, they should be killing the dangerous ones, like Z.

Getting out of his car, he glanced from the truck to the second floor. Would his new neighbor turn out to be an escaped subject, a human, or a natural-born menace?

He'd soon find out since he'd hit her place for DNA before she finished work. To ensure she didn't wake him, he slid a note under her door. He listened to see if he'd hear her dog.

Was it the hypersensitive type that barked at everything? The silent but deadly kind that would chew off his leg before he could say, "Good doggie"?

Maybe he could bribe it. He had a package of ham-flavored tofu.

He would figure it out later. For the next few hours, his pillow had his name written all over it. He didn't get as much sleep as he'd hoped.

## CHAPTER 4

**DEAR DIARY: LAST NIGHT I HAD THE ODDEST DREAM.**

Dreaming for me wasn't unusual. I've got a vivid imagination, and it drove my parents nuts during my younger years, especially when I went through my aliens-seeded-this-planet-and-started-humanity phase. I was convinced ETs chose monkeys and blended their DNA with them. Had to be. And I'd had this conviction before I even discovered how abnormal my own genetic strand was. Could I be of extra-terrestrial origin? An alien egg artificially inseminated with human DNA with me as the result?

My parents refuted the idea, but they also never had an answer to my actual parentage. Dinosaur? Possibly. My tail definitely screamed reptile.

But back to my dream. I was in a dark place. Think super pit of nothingness and multiply that by freaky.

Did I mention I don't like the dark?

My voice emerged with a tremor. "Hello?"

It echoed and then abruptly stopped, as if someone threw a muffling blanket over it. Not unnerving at all.

I sucked my lower lip as I turned to see if there was any difference around me. The lack of anything, even sound, pressed on me. Could I be crushed by nothingness?

I didn't intend to find out. This was *my* dream. Time to own it. "Let me go," I snapped and shoved back at the darkness trying to smother me.

To my surprise, the pressure eased. A shadow moved, the noise of it much like leaves in a soft breeze.

"Hello?" I wished it could have had a firmer, more confident tone. Hard to feel brave when your knees wanted to knock.

A voice emerged from all around me. "Who are you?" Low, shivery, scary.

Add in the fact that from a very young age my mother taught me to not talk to strangers, I countered, "Who are you?"

"A prisoner." Spoken with a definite grumble. The timbre of it deep and delicious. I could have masturbated to that voice.

The very idea almost had me giggling. Probably not the best thing with a guy admitting he was in prison.

"Why are you in jail?" I asked. "Are you a prisoner of war? Or state? A prisoner of society and its rules? Or are you being persecuted for your beliefs?" A science brain always wanted to know everything. It meant I could, at times, ask a lot of questions.

Not everyone appreciated it.

"Silence," the guy I'd yet to see boomed.

"Don't you shush me. This is my dream," I countered.

"This isn't a dream but a nightmare, my nightmare, and I don't know why you're here to torture me."

"How am I torturing you?" I retorted.

"Because this darkness is all I can have. They won't let me wake. They keep me locked inside with only my thoughts to keep me company."

"They, who?" Because I was curious. What kind of conspiracy theory had my dream conjured?

"The doctors. The scientists. All those who fear my greatness."

I snorted. "You were doing okay until the greatness part."

"You doubt me?"

"No, but aren't we all great in some respects?"

"Some are much greater than others."

"Can't be that great if you're a prisoner."

"Don't mock me," he growled, which had he been a rabid dog or raccoon would have been scary; however, he was a disembodied voice in the dark and inside my dream.

This was my head. My weird sleeping reality.

I laughed. "You have to admit your claim is strange. If you are a prisoner, then how are you talking to me?"

"You tell me. How did you get inside? In all my

wandering I've not yet found a door. Not even a wall. Just endless darkness."

"Then imagine one. This is a dream. Anything is possible."

"Apparently it's possible for me to be even more irritated than I am already." The annoyance huffed around me, not hot or cold, and yet I shivered.

"Don't get pissy with me," I retorted, fighting my fear. "I'm not the one that stuck you in here."

"Are you though? Or are you just a voice sent to taunt me? To torture?"

"You're the one with no body. I'm right here." I glanced down to see myself, and I knew it was a dream because I wore real jeans and a T-shirt, not a lumpy skirt. Because, in this reality, I could hide my tail.

"I don't see you. Show yourself."

"Wow. Aren't you a little demanding? How about you show yourself first?"

"Do you really want to see?" The darkness shifted. The shadow swirled to take shape, rustling like dry leaves before a cold pre-winter breeze. A huge figure towered, impossibly wide, menacing—

*Beep. Beep. Beep.*

My alarm went off, and I woke suddenly, my eyes flashing open. The dream ended, and I was a little pissed. I kind of wanted to see what my mind conjured to go with that sexy voice.

Maybe I could continue the dream tonight.

*Underground, in a medical facility...*

*Blip. Blip. Blip.* The heightened brain activity rang some bells and brought technicians running to stare at the screen and Subject Z, still asleep in his bed.

"Is he waking up?

A hand hovered over the emergency button.

The waves subsided.

False alarm.

"Should we call Ben?"

"Nah. He just left. Let him sleep. We'll keep watch."

But Subject Z didn't move. He plotted in the darkness.

## CHAPTER 5

DEAR DIARY: I START MY NEW JOB TODAY.
WISH ME LUCK.

Before I'd even had a cup of coffee, I saw a note that someone had slid under my door "Not working today. Not feeling good. Ben."

Not feeling good? Odd, because I'd heard the hum of his car—which probably used a hamster wheel under the hood—and seen it leave late at night. It hadn't returned by the time I'd gone to bed.

Him not going in suited me fine. It gave me time to calm my nerves. Nothing would happen. I was just a lowly lab tech—who was going to spy and see if I could find signs they were a Frankenstein lab, mixing and matching parts.

Fingers crossed I didn't get caught.

I drove the beast to my new job, having chosen to wear an ankle-length pleated skirt, my tail stuffed into my big-booty undies, the kind meant to give me some shape. The term baby's got back? I had back, side, under, over. You could sit a tray on it. It attracted the wrong sort all the time.

No, I was not into anal sex. And no, I didn't want to smother them, not even for fifty bucks.

I parked the beast at the back of the lot fifteen minutes before start time. There were only about a two dozen employees there. I followed them to the building, cement with tinted windows, green space around it kept trimmed except for a flowerbed, where bright blooms spelled out CTI.

The employees streamed for the bank of doors, two sets. I followed the shortest looking line. I stepped inside and felt something. A jolt that shuddered through me. Apparently, I wasn't alone.

"Shit. Was that a mini quake?" someone exclaimed.

The lobby was the kind with shiny tile floors and plastic chairs bolted down. The first level was the collection floor. Lots of money to be made when contracted with the government. Since the pandemic, the lab had apparently been working nonstop. Was even finally discussing plans to create a second building alongside the first.

"Do we need to take cover?"

I listened to the comments being tossed around. Other people who'd arrived early like me. The clinic would open at nine. Since ours didn't do the fasting tests, there wasn't a lineup or a need to open earlier.

"I think it's stopped," replied the guard who'd come from around his desk.

Were they sure? Because I still felt kind of wobbly. Could be because I was nervous. I'm not nervous, you're nervous.

Humor. It fell flat even in my head.

My stomach clenched. So much could go wrong. As I brushed my teeth this morning, I'd begun thinking about what would happen if I got caught spying. A company who experimented with humans, against all laws, might not have a problem eradicating anyone who got in their way.

I could end up dead in the worst-case scenario.

But...on the other hand...

If what I read in the box of lies was true, then what they did to me was just the start. The box lacked details, but what it implied... Horrible. I could imagine some pretty bad shit.

The box made it clear I wasn't a fluke of nature. Someone had made me. It didn't say if I was created in a test tube or the result of something horrific like rape. I really hoped my creation came about as a milkshake version—a touch of this, a dab of that, and shake it all about.

The box didn't mention my bio parents, but it did go into detail about other things.

Why did my mom and dad—those wretched liars —*Oh how I miss you*—have to leave me that box?

If they loved me as they claimed, why did they

shred my world? The familiar anguish clenched me just as the lights in the building flickered.

Which led me to head toward the security guard and ask, "Is this building safe?" Earthquake, power fluctuations. Signs I should turn around and never look back?

The portly fellow wearing a black shirt and pants, straining at the seams, offered a shrug. "That's been happening for a few days now. Corp is supposed to get someone in to check on it."

"And the earthquake? Does it happen often?" I asked.

"That would be our first."

"Oh good," I tittered because tittering women were never taken seriously. The guard checked me out and hiked his drooping pants.

"Yeah, we don't really get quakes," he said, suddenly thinking he had an avid audience.

"A good thing given a loss of power would surely be bad for the delicate samples handled here."

"No need to worry. We've got gennies to back us up if the power goes out."

"Good to know."

"Speaking of knowing, how can I help you? You're early for the clinic. They don't open until nine." He smiled.

I returned it as I lightly said, "I'm the new lab tech. I was told to present myself at the desk."

"Let me check my list." He rounded the counter.

"Name?" he asked, tapping the screen on the tablet lying atop his counter.

"Kalini Johnson." I used my parents' last name but wasn't too worried. Johnson was one of the most common last names out there. And not the one my parents had when they worked for CTI.

He typed in my name and then eyed the picture and then me. He offered a short nod. "Yup. All good. You'll want to take the elevator to level two."

"Is that up or down?"

"There's only an up," he stated.

I knew that was a lie. I'd studied the plans. Noticed how the older surveys showing a cavern system at that address had been replaced by a solid ground indication. A pretty big change.

Unless you were hiding something.

"This will allow you access to the places you're authorized." The security guard handed me a card already printed with my name and face. My security clearance. The lowest-level version. I'd have to upgrade it.

"Thanks."

"Carl. Name is Carl." He beamed.

I managed a short smile then headed off, knowing Carl was staring at my ass. Let him look. His interest might help me later.

Stepping into the elevator, I noticed the number pad with buttons for the main floor, plus floors two to five. Yet, research on this place showed it had been built atop a previous building that had a massive basement level. Was it unused?

I jabbed two.

*Ding.* The doors shut. The elevator had no music, a refreshing change. It barely made a sound as it whooshed up a single floor. It opened into a place packed with about a dozen cubicles, each containing the tools needed for testing. Most of it was automated, but they still needed a human to press some buttons and insert the samples. And that was the part most prone to messing up.

No wonder we were getting replaced by robots.

Someone with a clipboard spotted me. It didn't take long to meet my new boss, get assigned a station, and get started on some samples. You would think everyone arriving at eight would cause chaos. Instead it was a well-oiled machine, with everyone getting scheduled breaks that included a large coffee with two creams and six sugars delivered to my desk. Catered lunch buffet-style meant I could eat a plate from it and then snack all day long on the stash of meat sticks I'd brought.

It was an awesome day of work. I could totally get into the groove so long as I didn't find out they were still experimenting on people.

At five, people packed up and left, saying goodbye, reminding me not to linger.

Oh, I lingered, mostly to see how long it would take for someone to notice. At 5:06 someone in a uniform arrived on level two. Not Carl. This fellow didn't smile at me at all.

"Ma'am, it's quitting time."

"But I'm almost done," I said, looking away from my screen for a second.

"You'll have to finish tomorrow. Corp has a strong policy when it comes to hours of operation."

"Okay. Sorry. New here. I'll grab my stuff and go."

He waited while I put on my coat and grabbed my purse. He even escorted me to the elevator, but he didn't get on with me.

Made me wonder why they were so strict about quitting time. Did something happen here at night and they didn't want anyone to know?

It made me decide to come back later. Because something about this place niggled at me. It was more than just the fact I quavered inside the whole time I was in that building. I could tell it had a secret even if I'd seen nothing untoward.

Could be, after what happened in the lab that burned, they'd learned their lesson. Turned to the straight and narrow. Stopped playing with lives.

Call it a gut feel, but I didn't think CTI was lily white.

As the elevator hit the first floor, I glanced down at my feet. The elevator's machinery was probably in the basement. Going down would require stairs. Tomorrow, I'd use the stairs to climb to the second floor and see if they went down as well.

As I strutted—my tail butt bouncing behind me—I could have sworn the ground shivered.

I wrapped my coat closer. *No earthquakes my ass, Carl.*

---

BLIP. *Blip. Blip.*

The lab that once went months without anything of note scrambled to stay ahead of Subject Z's increased brain activity. Despite the drugs, all day long he showed signs of being awake inside there.

His body didn't move. Still, a sense of nervousness filled everyone who worked with Z. None of them wanted to be around if he ever woke up. They all remembered what happened the last time his consciousness swam to the surface. The first person to barf started a chain reaction.

"Where's Ben?" asked Kiara. "Does he know what's going on?"

"He'll be in for the third shift. Said he was handling something."

"He should be handling this." The nervousness in her voice was something they all felt.

Maybe it was time to put Subject Z into the last sleep.

The one that would ensure he never woke up and destroyed the world.

## CHAPTER 6

DEAR DIARY: I CAME HOME TO FIND
MURPHY OUTSIDE. I HAVE NO IDEA HOW,
BUT HE SEEMS TO HAVE DISCOVERED A WAY
AND BURIED MY HAIRBRUSH AND NEW
TOOTHBRUSH SOMEWHERE IN THE YARD.

AFTER TAKING care of my dog and chastising him —"Bad, Murphy. No opening my door and hiding my shit"—I took him for a walk. Gagged at his epic poop and then brought him home for a feeding. He'd now sleep until morning.

A good thing because my plan involved driving past the entrance for CTI a few times. I didn't spot a camera, but that didn't mean shit. It could have been hiding in plain sight. If I pulled in to check the parking lot, would it be noticed? I couldn't afford to get discovered yet.

On one of my passes, I happened to see a car coming out of the company drive, waiting to turn onto the road.

Coincidence? Maybe someone doing a U-turn because they were lost?

I yawned. This wasn't helping me at all. What I should do was buy one of those cameras that could record movement and put it on one of the trees overlooking the company parking lot.

Returning to my apartment, I discovered Murphy taking up the whole bed. By elbowing and shoving, and conceding to sleep on an angle with one foot on the floor, I managed to fall asleep.

This time when my dream started in that dark place, I was ready. I'd had all day to imagine what the shadow in my head could be. My favorite? Dragon. I knew they didn't exist. After much study I concluded that the stories about them probably originated because of a dinosaur that lasted longer than the rest.

Still…when I wanted to feel good about the world and myself, I used to pretend I was a dragon. Because it made everything better.

I planted my hands on my hips and shouted to the darkness pressing against me, "Show yourself."

A rustle let me know he listened.

"I know you're there. Why are you hiding?"

"You ask that of me and yet I don't see you."

"I'm right here." I willed myself to appear, and I heard him suck in a breath.

A shadow didn't breathe, surely?

It could however mock. "There you are, wearing a benign face. Why won't you show your true self?" The voice curled around me, and rather than recoil, I warmed to it.

"You mean my tail? Fine. Here it is." It took but a thought to change to what I saw in the mirror every day. The jeans were replaced by a loose muumuu. My tail peeked out from under the edge.

"What kind of trickery is that?"

"No trick. This is me."

"It's a mockery of who you are."

"As if you know what I am," I scoffed. Was it weird to argue with a dream personality I'd created?

"Where are your horns? Your wings?"

I gaped at him. "I don't have any. Bad enough trying to camouflage my tail. If had horns or wings, I might as well go hide in the mountains until I die."

"What's wrong with mountains? I've always been partial to them. Less people."

I opened and shut my mouth before admitting, "Actually, I like mountains. The point is, my life is hard enough hiding my tail, so I don't need anyone, not even a dream-voice hunk, wishing more on me."

"Dream voice?" The low chuckle tickled.

"I know this isn't real."

"You are both right and wrong about that. It exists outside of the solid world but is very much real."

"How come you won't show yourself?"

"And which face would you have me show you?"

"You have more than one?"

"So do you."

I wanted to argue, but it was true. We wore the faces we needed. "Which one do you prefer?"

"The one that sends people screaming. You should try it sometime."

"Making people scream isn't really my thing."

"Are you sure?" he asked. "Because when done right, it can result in delightful things." He finally emerged from the shadows, the massive width of him shrinking down to normal size. A man, taller than me, Mediterranean in appearance, with his dark hair flowing in layers. His body was wide but lean. His eyes were a laser-cutting blue. Lips a flat, rigid line that smirked. Beautiful and cruel in one.

Totally out of my league. At least my imagination had good taste.

"Aren't you pretty," I drawled. It was easy to be confident when you knew it wasn't real. "You're more normal looking than expected."

"You're the one who chooses to mix and match parts. Is it for attention?" he accused.

"You think I wanted to be born with this?" I pointed to the spaded end peeking under the hem of my gown. "This is not a costume accessory."

"Put it away."

I snorted. "Sure, let me just pop it off and put it in a drawer. It doesn't come off. It doesn't go away. The best I can do is hide it and hope no one notices." I had this anxiety that upon my death, they'd find it and put me on display like some freak instead of cremating me.

"You have no idea who you are. Or what." His cruel expression softened into curiosity. It didn't last as he snapped, "Who are your parents? What is your lineage?"

He threw questions at me, and I had no answers. I shrugged. "I don't know, but finding out is why I moved and started the new job. And since you're a dream construct, you know that. So why are you asking?" I mused aloud. Could it be that my subconscious via dream was emphasizing the importance of answering the question about my roots?

Dream hunk paced, grace in his movements, along with a snap of violence. He bristled with it. "Where are you working?"

"CTI. Chymera Tech Industries."

He pivoted to stare at me. "Are you stupid? Do you know what they'll do if they find out about you?"

"Fire me?"

"You'll be lucky if you walk out alive. More likely they'll capture you."

"And do what? Lock me in a cage for testing?" I tried mocking, and yet it emerged breathy.

"They've usually got a few empty ones in the basement. We'd almost be roommates."

"You said before that you were a prisoner. What kind of prisoner? And when you say basement, you're talking about the one at CTI HQ?"

"Yes, I am a few levels below ground, I think. It's hard to tell anything. Even time passing. What is the year?"

I told him.

His brow furrowed. "It can't have been that long. It

would mean years lost. Years that no one has found me." His jaw hardened.

"They know how to hide their tracks." They'd been doing it since before my birth.

"They are also connected. Organized. It's how they caught me. But I will escape." He glanced upward as if he could see past the dark.

It made me wonder if my dream guy considered my head a prison. Was he some inward manifestation of my frustration trying to escape?

"What will you do if you get out of the basement?" I asked.

"I'll come find you." Ominous words and suddenly he was right in front of me.

I gaped. "Me? Why me?"

"Because you are the one able to step inside my prison. The one making it possible for me to finally break free."

"I haven't done anything."

"You're here"—he leaned into my space—"reminding me what it means to live."

He was close enough I could have kissed him.

It was a dream, so I did. I pressed my mouth to his and heard his sharp inhalation. Felt the rigid shock that tensed his frame. Was my frustration actually sex related? Maybe, because dream hunk was suddenly kissing me back and lighting me on fire, dragging me onto my tiptoes and plundering my mouth.

His hands groped me, and I let him. I'd tucked my

tail away and was ready and willing for him to hike my leg and take me.

Something pulsed in the darkness, and he tore his mouth from mine, growling, "No. No, you won't take this from me."

The pulsing increased and became unpleasant, enough that I woke, my heart pounding with an insistent throb between my legs. If only he were real.

---

"WHAT THE FUCK? Does he have a hard-on?" Ben stared at it, tenting the sheet over Subject Z.

"How is that even possible?" Kiara exclaimed.

Too many faces pressed against the glass, eyeing the astonishing sight of Subject Z and his boner.

"He's stirring," stated Kiara.

"Increase his dosage," barked Ben.

"We did. It's not working. Oh shit, his hands are flexing." The high-pitched exclamation had Jerome, with a brand-new baby at home, backing from the window.

Ben remained planted in place. "Up the sleeping drug."

"We've already increased it five percent," Kiara said.

"Up it again, he's moving!" someone shouted.

"I'm out of here!" The statement caused a panicked rush for the elevator. No one wanted to be left in the room when the emergency button was pressed.

They all couldn't cram aboard in one trip. Ben let the cowards leave and watched with crossed arms.

"Up it some more." He wouldn't lose, not today. Not to a monster.

"But..."

Ben whirled and snapped at Kiara, "Up it or I'll toss you to him when he breaks out of his shackles."

"Yes, sir."

In the end they increased his sleeping drugs by almost twenty-seven percent. Only then did Z slip back into a zone where the machines barely blipped.

It had been close. Too close.

Ben monitored for the next few hours, but everything remained quiet. He sent in a report. With the bolded line, **Highly recommend: termination.**

The reply? No.

"Idiots." Disgusted, Ben went home. It probably saved his life.

## CHAPTER 7

DEAR DIARY: I REALLY NEED TO BUY SOME BATTERIES.

Waking up horny wasn't my idea of a good time. I'd have preferred to have my weird dream hunk finish the job and give me a fake, yet still satisfying, little O. Now instead I was awake too early, with my hand in my underwear, rubbing my clit like I could find a genie.

I didn't get three wishes. Instead, I brought myself to orgasm, shaking and shivering, my eyes closed as I pictured my dream hunk as the one pleasuring me. Pure fantasy since I'd never get a guy like that in real life, someone who would accept me tail and all. Although, in my dream, he'd accused me of cherry-picking my parts.

If I was going to create extra limbs, it would be a boob, or another arm. All more useful than my tail. Three boobs, I could have been an exotic dancer and made a fortune before I turned thirty.

I showered and dressed quickly, letting Murphy outside to do his business. I was lucky he was such a low energy dog. His needs were simple: eat, sleep, and crush me when he decided he wanted in my lap. The fact he outweighed me never crossed his meathead brain. He heard thunder and boom! I had a lap dog.

By seven thirty, I headed downstairs, only to see my neighbor's car already gone. Thank fuck. I'd dodged the ride-sharing bullet two days in a row, which suited me just fine.

I cranked the tunes, heavy metal to get my blood pumping. It went well with my road raging tendencies. Cut me off? I'd flash my lights and make you think I was pulling you over. In the left lane? Then either find your gas pedal or get out of the way. If they didn't, I crawled up their asses. My big truck always intimidated. If it took them particularly long, I sometimes gave them the finger as I passed.

Never mistake me for docile. I might have to hide parts of me, but that didn't make me a pushover. The road ahead cleared, and I made really good time. I'd discovered that while people weren't encouraged to stay late, we could technically start showing up any time after seven. It helped stagger the arrival of employees, apparently. I arrived at ten to eight, a respectable time for the new girl. Probably the busiest as well, which meant I blended right in with the people getting out of their cars and doing the shuffle to the front door. The morning types smiled and waved. The normal ones kept their gazes averted and clutched at their coffee as if it were the only thing keeping them sane.

A tingle went through me as I got close to the building, but no tremors. Not that anyone noticed at any rate. I kept looking down as if the pavement were the most interesting thing.

It wasn't, in case anyone wondered.

We funneled into the building, the tighter quarters meaning I nodded and offered a few tight smiles. Fit in, become a regular fixture, and no one would notice me poking around the building. I wanted a better feel for the layout. Discover how deep their security went. Check out those stairs and see if they happened to go down. Look for a basement where dream hunk claimed he was being held prisoner.

Dream hunk didn't exist, and yet I had to wonder if his claim was my subconscious trying to poke me about something I might have seen or heard. Something significant enough I was dreaming about it.

It should be easy enough to find out if this place had a basement. If it did, I'd take a peek and satisfy my curiosity.

My plans didn't exactly work out. The moment I sat at my desk the lights flickered. I glanced at them. We didn't exactly have great daylight in our cubicles, and we needed computers to work.

I placed my stuff on my chair and then went for the washroom. It wasn't eight o'clock yet, and the bathroom proved a popular place. As I sat and rid myself of two cups of coffee, making room for more, I listened. There was some boring chatter about what two of them were making for dinner. I was wiping when one of them said, "They're using this place after hours, but no one knows for what."

"How do you know?" gasped the friend in proper shock.

"Gary. The other night, when he was outside having a smoke, he saw two people leaving from a side door."

"Cleaning crew?"

"Nope." The gossiper popped her P. "He knows the cleaning crew, and it wasn't them. Turns out he doesn't even have a key for that door. When he asked the boss about it, he got written up because he was smoking on company property."

"That's so rude," exclaimed the friend.

Actually, more ironic than rude. It was made clear no smoking was allowed on company grounds.

"Right?" said the gossiping woman. "Anyhow, they told him to forget what he saw, and reminded him of his confidentiality clause."

"They are definitely up to something crooked."

In this case they were correct. That definitely sounded as if something hinky was happening.

As I exited the stall, I felt another tremor. I stuck my arms out to balance, and the women who were about to leave ogled me.

"Did you feel that?" That was my weak query.

"No."

"Must have been a ghost tremor." I smiled. They returned a polite one and left.

As I washed my hands, I glanced at myself in the mirror. Why did I imagine I felt the building shaking? Did I need to be worrying about my health?

My new bangs were too short because I'd cut them while my hair was wet, thinking I'd accounted for how much they'd shrink when dry. I didn't. They were slanted across the top of my brows, but they did at least cover the pushing nubs on my forehead. Was I seriously about to grow some horns? As if hiding a tail weren't difficult enough. I huffed in annoyance as I shoved my hands under the blower to dry them.

The machine came on, and my hands flexed. The blower exploded and blew me backward.

I gasped in shock more than pain as I hit the floor. The lights buzzed and then went out, leaving me lying on my back in the darkness.

I rose to my elbows then sat up completely. That had been quite the zap. How did my hair look? Like I'd shoved a finger into a socket? Had it been badly singed? It was my one pride and joy. Long, silky, thick. I didn't worry much about my bangs given my hair grew easily and quickly. I trimmed a few inches every two weeks.

The lights didn't return, so I felt my way to the door, hoping it didn't suddenly open.

It did, but luckily only glanced off my shoulder. I

managed not to fall, but I did hiss and pulled a vampire as a flashlight shone in my face.

"We need to evacuate," the wielder of the light stated.

"What happened to the power?" I asked, following him into the corridor. At the far end, an Exit sign glowed in the shadows.

"It went out."

I almost snapped, *Thank you, Captain Obvious.* Instead I went with a gentler, "Probably because of the tremor."

"Most likely."

As he went to herd me to the exit, I dug in my heels. "I need to get my jacket and purse."

"We gotta leave."

"It will literally take thirty seconds, and there's a traffic jam at the stairs." Indeed, the employees had formed a file to go down.

"Be quick."

I was not offered the flashlight. A good thing I'd memorized the path from the bathroom to lab number thirteen.

I grabbed my stuff but then kept going to the opposite side of the building where schematics had shown there should be a second staircase. Why did no one use them?

I made it to the hall, which had another pair of washrooms but no exit sign. There was, however, a door. The handle was locked, and no amount of jiggling loosened it.

"Hey, wrong way."

"Is it?" I tittered as I whirled. "I'm new and wasn't sure where to go."

I received a personal escort across to the other side, and I couldn't help but wonder, why the intense security? And what was up with the power?

Each step I took, I had to resist an urge to turn around. I watched my feet. Stared at the floor. Could have sworn it roiled, and yet no one stumbled or cried out. The very air held a portent that lifted the hairs on my neck.

*Crack.*

The streak of lighting—a sizzling purple and yellow streak—hit a car in the lot.

"Holy fuck!" I wasn't the only one to exclaim. It was kind of cool unless you owned the damaged car.

That person cried.

But as more lightning hit the ground, people screamed and scattered.

Weird that the sky had not a single cloud in it. Where did the electricity come from?

And why wasn't I scared?

I made it to my truck unscathed, and by then the weird storm had ceased. But people fled as if they'd fry any second.

The lightning stopped about a mile away. Freaky and super rare according to research. I went to bed early, crosswise along the foot of my bed since Murphy had slobbered on my pillows.

I tossed and turned, my dreams chaotic, full of fire and lightning. Danger. Fear.

Dream hunk didn't appear. I was disappointed.

---

All night long they battled to keep Subject Z subdued. They'd doubled his sleeping sedative and increased the power on the fields to contain him. Nothing was working. He kept pushing past all their barriers.

Ben called his boss twice to ask for permission to terminate.

He was refused.

At dawn, they lost the battle.

## CHAPTER 8

DEAR DIARY: I HAVE NOTHING TO SAY. IT'S TOO EARLY.

I AWOKE with a jolt at dawn.

Yes, fucking dawn, which this time of the year was before six. An ungodly hour. Even my dog wouldn't budge.

A coffee did help make me feel a touch more human. My shower had me sighing in pleasure. But I really woke up when I bit into the toaster strudel with the extra Betty Crocker icing. Okay, it was four strudels, and I didn't regret a single one.

My dog eventually sauntered out and left to do his business. I dressed for work. Having not received a call or email saying otherwise, I assumed I should go in.

I left Murphy with a clean toilet, water in the sink, and a rack of ribs I'd bought on sale and cooked for him last night.

No sign of my neighbor. I now began to wonder if he regretted mentioning the carpool thing and was avoiding me. I really should get a look inside his place one of these days. He was pretty high up in the company. Maybe he had some dirt.

As I neared my place of work, flashing lights appeared in my rearview mirror. As if seeing it triggered my hearing, the wail of a siren caught up. Being a law-abiding citizen who never wanted to be strip searched, I pulled over onto the shoulder and stopped. A fire truck flew by me. Then another, their sirens and lights going off, as they rushed to a scene.

As I watched them scream past, I glanced into the sky and saw a curl of smoke. Close to my work it appeared. Had yesterday's lightning started a fire in the forest around the property?

With no more fire trucks coming, I pulled back onto the road, passing a line of trees that only broke at the wide entrance to my work. A glance to the sky showed billowing smoke.

Apparently, I wasn't the only one to come into work. I ran into crawling traffic as we approached the company's subtle signage consisting of the CTI logo—the winged griffon-lion thing with the number 666. I had to wonder if that last part was intentional.

The moment I turned in, I knew it was CTI on fire. What surprised me was no one was stopping us from getting in. While the fire trucks had arrived, the police hadn't. A car just ahead of me proceeded to do the most awkward U-turn and sped away. Others, like me, went forward, our nature demanding we gawk and find out what had happened. Deny it however much you wanted; within many exists a firebug that wants to see stuff burn.

The two lanes were bordered by trees, so I couldn't see much. It didn't help that three-quarters in, we had to inch because of cars that had pulled to the side and the people who had spilled out and were gawking. Drones, who stared in stunned shock as smoke poured from the building. Firemen on the ground had hooked up their hoses and were heading for the main doors. With no room at the curb, I pulled into the back end of our parking lot and reversed into a spot under a tree. I got out of my vehicle and hugged myself as I stared at the burning building. The smoke tickled my noise. Even from here, I could feel the heat.

Was the arson a coincidence? I'd not done anything yet that could have triggered any alarms. This had to be an accident, caused by either the earthquake or the lightning of the day before. Heck, it could have been the electrical issue that shut us down.

There were a few more cars in the lot, their drivers standing beside them, some of them holding up their phones. I saw one wearing a flowered mask, probably a remnant from the pandemic in 2020. I moved close to someone I vaguely recalled seeing the day before and said, "What happened?"

The woman, wearing glasses, a pixie haircut, and an avid expression, appeared shocked. "I heard there was a gas explosion in one of the labs. It's exploded a few more times since."

Not what I'd expected. Worse. The building would be a total loss. There went my chance for answers. My only hope, which was faint at this point, was off-site records or that the company had a backup online somewhere. If such records existed, I'd have to find them or admit defeat about my past.

Maybe this was a sign that I should stop digging.

"This sucks so bad. I needed that medical insurance." This would be a devastating blow to everyone who worked here.

As I was about to leave, someone standing farther ahead with a group of people turned. My neighbor, Ben, had a scowl and looked downright disheveled. His gaze tracked over those watching until they hit me. He headed over, and I met him halfway.

"Sorry. I should have left a note telling you to stay home."

"What happened?" If anyone knew or had a bullshit story, it would be Ben. Online company portfolio listed him as being in charge of public relations.

"Gas explosion." He confirmed the rumor. "The leak must have happened overnight. Someone came in early and smelled it. Unfortunately, something sparked it before we could have it shut off and drained from the building."

Super plausible. "Was anyone hurt?"

And this was when his expression flickered. Just for a teeny, tiny second his face changed. I blinked, and it was gone. In its place was a perfectly sad mien as he said, "We are praying no one was inside."

Me too. "Did the gas start leaking in the basement? Happened to a neighbor of mine," I added as he gave me a sharp look.

"There is no basement." Flatly spoken.

I didn't believe him. Not that it mattered anymore.

The building erupted. Like *kaboom*! Everyone hit the ground screaming.

I hit the pavement and covered my head. Because that would totally protect me from falling debris.

Sarcasm. It helped with my fear.

The yelling as the firemen adapted their strategy penetrated my daze. A hand grabbed me by the arm. Ben yanked me to my feet. "You should go home."

"Yeah." I didn't want to be around when they found out if human smelled like bacon or chicken when cooking.

"I'll come by in a bit."

He would? "Why?"

"To check on you."

"But I'm fine." I blew him off, only to realize he might be my last link to CTI. "You'll probably be hungry though. I'll make you some brownies."

"Okay. I'll be there shortly."

I hustled back to my truck, opening the door, coughing at the smoke that swirled past me. Ugh. This was why I could never smoke cigarettes. Although I didn't mind a good pot vape.

I put the air on recirculate the second I started the engine. I didn't want to bring in any outside air until I got clear. The filter would remove most of the smoke. I hoped. It still tickled.

Pulling out of the lot, I got stuck behind the other gawkers who just had to slow down even more and crane as the cops finally arrived. One car even pulled around and went back to watch some more.

Once I emerged out of the bottleneck driveway, I managed to put on some speed. Only then with the fresher air did I open the windows and let my truck have a cabin full of the clean stuff before closing them again.

Ah. Much better. I took a deep breath. Exhaled. Another...

My throat felt better, but my stomach grumbled. By now I'd usually have delved into my snack stash. Today, I had a cinnamon raisin pastry with icing sugar.

Mmm. My tummy grumbled aloud. My snack was in the backseat, though.

"Shh. I'll feed you. Give me a second to find a place to park." Or even better, a spot to eat. As I drove, I gave my navigation verbal instructions.

"Find me a place to eat breakfast."

*"I'm sorry, I can't do that,"* replied a modulated female voice.

The battle was about to begin. Ever since I'd bought this truck, my Smart Navigation system had been thwarting me.

I hit the microphone and said slowly and succinctly, "Find me a restaurant."

*"What kind of restaurant?"*

"Breakfast."

*"Invalid entry. What kind of restaurant?"*

"Fast food." A drive-through would work. I loved crunchy hash browns.

*"Fast Food. With drive-through or without?"*

"With." As if there was any other kind.

*"With drive-through offering American fare, French cuisine, breakfast—"*

"Breakfast," I yelled. Finally. I just wanted waffles with strawberry syrup and home fries.

*"I'm sorry. I did not understand your selection. Session ended for inactivity."*

I blinked at my dash as I muttered, "I hate you."

"I think your truck hates you back," said a voice from my back seat.

## CHAPTER 9

DEAR DIARY: I ALMOST SHIT MY PANTS TODAY. GOOD THING MY SEATS ARE LEATHER.

I SCREAMED and jerked the wheel, kicking up dust on the gravelly shoulder of the road as I screeched to a halt. Someone was in my truck!

I remembered every single movie where someone died because of this scenario and screamed again. Then glanced in my mirror and realized my backseat held a big naked man. "What the fuck?"

Not just any man.

Dream hunk.

"I'm hallucinating," I declared. Or still sleeping. This was not happening.

"I'm real," he said, his voice raspy.

"Nope." I shook my head. He didn't go away or acquire clothes to hide those broad, naked shoulders.

I leaned my head on the steering wheel of my truck. Closed my eyes. Must be some kind of hallucinogenic effect due to smoke inhalation. I needed fresh air. Bzzzt. I rolled down the window and shoved my face out. I sucked in a ton of air. Inhaled it so hard it burned my nostrils, but I felt clear headed. My lungs clean.

Another glance at my mirror showed the naked hunk in my Suburban remained, and he had demands. "I'll need some clothes."

"You mean *I* need clothes. I'm pretty sure I sh—" I hastily change it to, "peed myself. How did you get inside my truck?" Because I surely would have noticed him on the drive in to work. Or would I? It took him doing a naked-guy-in-the-truck-pop for me to realize he was there.

"I climbed through the tail gate. You didn't lock it when you parked."

"No way." I shook my head. "I would have noticed. There's a light in the trunk."

"You were busy talking, and I handled it."

I slowly turned enough to see him in the flesh. So much flesh. How had he remained hidden? Not to mention I could smell him. Like nutmeg sprinkled on some hot, honey-sweetened milk on a cold winter night.

Mmm. The smoke must have concealed the scent before.

"Why are you in my truck? Where did you come from? Why are you in your birthday suit?" Was I about to be raped? I should have been more frightened.

"I'm naked because they didn't see fit to clothe me where they were keeping me prisoner."

"Whoa. That was a whole bunch of crazy in one sentence." As crazy as the sexiest guy I'd ever seen in the buff. A face with chiseled planes and brilliant dark-lashed eyes. Then his lips. I'd kissed those lips in my dream. Put my hands on those broad shoulders with the well-defined pecs, the abs, and... My cheeks heated as I averted my gaze. "You never said why you were in my truck."

"I told you I'd come find you."

"How could you tell me when this is the first time we've met?"

He arched a brow. "Are you still persisting in denying reality? This is our third meeting."

"Those other two were dreams." This had to also be a dream. So why did it feel so real?

"Those weren't dreams but another plane of consciousness."

"You are still sounding nuts, naked man."

"My name is Urion."

"I'm Kalini, and this is insane." I lay my face on the steering wheel and accidentally honked it. Almost needed new pants for real that time.

"Why do you persist in not believing? Do you only define your reality as physical touch? Because that seems rather confining and short sighted." He sounded arrogant.

"I'm a scientist. I like things that can be measured. Felt. Seen."

"Did you not see me in that other place? Did you not feel me?"

I'd definitely felt something. Had my longing brought him to life? Did I have the magic of creation?

Apparently, I asked this aloud because he snorted. "No, you did not make me."

"Yet you found yourself inexplicably compelled to seek me out. Why?" Because in stories, monsters went looking for their makers.

"I told you I would find you."

He had. In that dark place.

"Were you really held prisoner in CTI's basement?"

"I don't know their name, but I was in some kind of subterranean prison."

Which led me to ask, "Did you burn the place down?"

"No, but I would have if given a chance. I was only interested in escaping, so when I woke from my drugged coma, I went for the nearest exit. I didn't stop for clothes. Or even revenge."

"So you didn't kill anyone?"

"Only those that got in my way."

Now there were some serious serial killer words. I swallowed hard. "If you didn't set the fire, then who did?"

"I imagine the white-coat bastards did. Probably trying to cover their tracks."

"What tracks? How? Why?" I peppered him with

questions. I needed more data, and all he did was add to the confusion.

"You want answers, I will provide them, but not on an empty belly. I need food and fluids to drain the rest of their drugs." He grimaced.

"You also need clothes. Pretty sure there's laws against riding around naked in public."

"Fetch me some suitable attire then."

I arched a brow. "I am not fetching you shit."

"Very well. Nude, it is." He then proceeded to move through the seats into the front passenger side.

That brought a lot of naked man too close to my face. I saw his tight ass as it went by and wanted to take a bite.

Instead, I hopped out of the truck and headed for the trunk where I kept a spare bag of clothes. I always had a just-in-case bag. My parents had drilled it into me to have one from a young age, dad always saying, *"If it ever gets to be too dangerous, run."* I thought they were preparing me for zombies and never expected I might need it in real life.

I pulled out a T-shirt, very baggy pants, and flip flops. I returned to the driver seat and offered them.

He eyed the pile, and his lip curled. "I am not a buffoon."

"And I don't carry men's clothing in my truck. Wear it or don't. I'm going to eat." I slammed the truck into drive and had the satisfaction of jostling him.

He uttered a low, grumbly sound.

I dared a glance, and he glared.

Pissed at me for helping him? I shot him a finger. "If you don't like it, get out and walk."

"You're difficult."

"You mean I don't roll over and show you my belly?" I laughed. "Dude, I might look sweet, and you might have some preconception about me, but I will warn you right now; I'm not a pushover." Wallflower, yes. But only because I had to hide my tail.

"You don't seem to realize the danger in flaunting yourself."

"Flaunting?" I glanced at him then snorted. "You have seen how I dress, right? Does that look like I'm flaunting?"

"You intentionally sought employment with *them*." He curled his lips with disdain. "Put yourself right under their nose."

"What else could I do? I wanted answers."

"What could you have wanted to know that foolishly?"

As I pulled into a diner parking lot, I paused before saying, "I was trying to find out if I am a monster."

## CHAPTER 10

DEAR DIARY: IS BEING ABLE TO EAT ALL THE CAKE I LIKE WITHOUT GAINING A POUND A SUPERPOWER OR A CURSE?

THERE WERE things I could do that always set me apart. Healing faster. My ability to eat copious amounts of food.

On and off, my entire life I'd pondered, *Am I a monster?* Every time I enjoyed a piece of steak, still pink in the middle, I questioned if one day I'd want it raw. What about when rare turned to fresh from a kill? Would I become a ravenous carnivore?

There was no denying the changes in me as I got older. As my tail thickened and lengthened, I wondered how long before I couldn't hide it. What if it were discovered and someone tried to remove it from me for my own good? I'd seen it happen to people around the world. People supposedly carrying around thirty- and forty-pound tumors. Snipped off. Was it a relief to have it gone? Or would I forever mourn its loss?

Without my tail, who would I be?

Exiting the truck, and my naked dilemma, I adjusted my tail discreetly and stalked to the diner I'd seen from the road. Screw you, GPS, my hash brown radar still worked fine.

The place had a gravel parking lot serving a white-sided, single-story rectangle. Atop it, a hand-painted sign with stenciled letters read Jo's Grits. Christmas lights followed their loopy shape. I bet it was wonderfully tacky at night and had the kind of coffee that would sprout hair on a chest. This kind of place promised greasy deep-fried food, daily pies, and linoleum.

Inside, the smell of bacon and toast cooking filled me with delight. My belly was growling so badly. I always craved more sustenance during periods of stress.

I stressed a lot. Half my paycheck went to feeding me and my dog. I headed for a booth in the corner that still allowed a view out the window. It meant I saw Urion get out of my truck wearing my clothes. He should have appeared ridiculous, but nothing could diminish the powerful lines of his body or the smooth gait that rolled from his hips as he stalked for the diner.

Why did he have to be even hotter in the flesh? How the hell had I met him in a dream?

Holy shit, what had I gotten into? I didn't know, but for the first time since I discovered the box of lies, I felt a stirring out of my anger and despair. Excitement like I'd never imagined.

Urion entered the diner and didn't bother to look around. He made a beeline for me.

My girl parts quivered. I pressed my thighs tight and pretended to study the menu. He slid in across from me. "You're not a monster." He picked up where we left off.

"Are you?" Would a psychopath say yes? Could it be that simple? Could we stop murder sprees simply by confronting psychos with a direct question?

"Humans would say I'm a monster."

"Humans? Meaning you're not."

"We're not," he corrected.

I wanted to repute, but the waitress arrived and took our order. She poured some coffee to get us started. She also brought my muffin right away.

Given how Urion eyed it, I reluctantly offered a piece. He had, after all, just escaped the basement.

Alone once more, I found myself saying, "Why do humans hate you?"

"Because they can't control me. It bothers them, whereas I enjoy the irony."

"How is hatred ironic?"

"Because they made that which could destroy them."

"Made?" My heart stopped at the choice of word. Could it be? Had I finally found another like me?

"Don't sound dubious. They made you, too."

The confirmation hit me hard, and I swallowed.

"How can you claim that when you know nothing about me?"

Again, he lifted that stupid eyebrow of his. Said more in that tilt than any words could. "I'd say I'd know you better than most. How many are aware of your secret?"

When my parents lived, I could have said two. Now? I didn't lie. "Just you. Which is one too many."

"As if I'd tell the humans." His lips curled.

"Seems weird, you hating them so much when you look just like them."

"One must blend in to survive. I think of it as camouflage."

"If this isn't your real face, what do you look like?"

He leaned forward and said quite seriously, "The monster they're all afraid of. The one under the bed."

"Can you ever just answer a question? Like, hey, what do you look like, Urion?" I pitched my voice. "Like a glob of shadow with no eyes or face. That, I can picture."

He stared at her. "Glob of shadow isn't as daunting."

"Then how about smoke demon or killer shadow?"

His lips flattened. "Now you are mocking me."

I smiled. Sweetly. "Would I do that?"

He scowled. "Remind me why I'm helping you."

"Helping me?" I scoffed. "We both know you don't have a wallet, which means I'm paying for breakfast."

"If it makes you feel better, you probably won't be

touching your funds for a while. We'll have to go off grid if we're going to drop out of sight."

"Rewind and say that again. Because you sound like you're implying I'm going somewhere with you."

"You are. We're leaving town as soon as we've finished eating. Once we hit the next city over, we'll ditch your truck for something more discreet."

"First off, the truck stays with me. Two, when I'm done stuffing my face, I'm going home. You can feel free to do whatever." I was magnanimous with my hand wave. Leave, peasant. More food for me.

"Are you completely oblivious? You can't go home. They might be looking for you there."

"Who?"

"The same humans who captured me."

"I just told you no one knows about my extra parts." A tail, plus four extra chromosomes to be exact.

"Don't be so sure. You're not hard to spot."

"Says you," I grumbled. "Most people assume I'm pear shaped."

"The scent doesn't lie."

"What do I smell like?" I'd gone with the powder fresh antiperspirant this morning.

"You remind me of a summer storm."

I had no idea what that meant, but it sounded poetic. "And you smell like a pastry."

He arched a brow. "Did you just call me good enough to eat?"

I blushed. Surprising given I usually uttered the smart-ass remark. "I never said that."

"You didn't have to," was his cocky reply. Damn him.

Time to change the subject. "How long were you kept a prisoner?" A good place to start rather than his claim of being made, which I was pretty sure didn't start with "When two people love each other and want to make that love bigger…"

"Years." His chin ducked. "My own fault. They caught me when I partied a little too hard."

"Caught you how? How did they know you were special?" I'd yet to figure out exactly what that entailed. Urion could obviously slip into dreams. Did he have mental powers? Shit, did he have mind control? Would he make me do unspeakably dirty things to his body?

Mmm.

"They found me accidentally. They were actually going after a different target when they happened to see me drunk in an alley, fighting off some muggers. They quickly pivoted their trap and took me down. I awoke manacled to a bed."

"That's awful."

"Yes." He didn't ask for sympathy or start recounting how horrible it was. He leaned back and let the waitress serve us a breakfast that would add at least ten pounds. I'd have it worked off by lunch.

All the smells had me moaning. Delicious. I dug in.

We both did, with me inhaling food and enjoying the fact he didn't feel a need to comment on how much I ate.

People always claimed they meant well, but they'd look at my stacked portion and then would offer a snide, "Wow, guess you're hungry." Some offered a blunt, "Ever think of reducing your calories?" The pamphlets about diets and nutrition left in my workspace were especially passive aggressive.

*I'm not fat. I just have a big tail.*

It was as I sucked the orange slice on the edge of my plate that I saw a familiar car pulling into the lot. Ben's little clown car. He parked it beside my truck and got out. He had his phone to his ear and scanned the parking lot, starting with my truck, before eyeballing the restaurant.

Was my neighbor spying on me? Probably just Urion's comments making me paranoid. Why would Ben be interested in me? I was a nobody. A nothing on his radar. Except he'd warned me he'd be checking up on me.

No need to warn Urion we were about to have company. He'd already slid out of the booth and angled himself out of sight of the window.

"I take it Ben seeing you is a bad thing," I said, reaching for his plate, dumping it onto mine, and sliding it under another to hide it. I drained his coffee and put it on my side too. Now it looked like a person with a huge appetite ate here.

"We need to leave."

"You're the one who has to go. It's not me he's after."

"Kalini..." He said my name, and for a second, I wavered.

Mind control. He was trying to make me do something I shouldn't.

"I'm not going with you. But I can stall him." Before Urion could argue, I headed for the cash register by the door. My waitress stood beside it counting someone's change. It didn't take her long to ring up my order, the total being as cheap as I'd hoped. I tossed two twenties on her counter.

"Keep the change." I was turning just as Ben entered.

I pasted a fake smile. "Imagine running into you again."

"You're here alone?" He gave away so much with that one query.

I didn't dare peek to see if Urion had gotten away.

"Yup. Thought I'd have a big breakfast before heading home. Terrible what happened."

"Very. The fire has destroyed everything, and now I'm hearing it might be arson."

"No?!" I tried to sound properly horrified.

"It's something they're looking at, which is why we're asking if anyone saw any strangers close to the fire this morning."

"Everyone's a stranger still to me." The high laugh

almost made me wince. I couldn't have sounded more inauthentic if I tried.

"True." He eyed the diner. "Thought you were going home?"

"I was but then let my stomach talk me into stopping. Don't worry. I'm still going to make those brownies. But they might be a few hours. I need to hit the grocery store before I make them. You should have some breakfast. I recommend the waffles. They are to die for. Later." I headed past him and did my best to walk rather than run.

My truck wasn't parked as discreetly this time, meaning no trees Urion could use as cover. Also, I'd locked it. Still, when I got in the truck, I checked the row behind. Empty. I lifted my butt off the seat and checked the cargo area.

No sign of a big man.

Surely, I wasn't disappointed?

---

URION COULDN'T WAIT for nightfall to move, and the effort took a toll. His time with those white-coat bastards had made him so weak. His fault for being so stupid. He knew to never let his guard down. The mistake cost him years and who knew what else. He'd been at their mercy. A subject for their tests.

At least he'd survived. Escaped their clutches. And

all because something woke him up, something energized him enough he could act.

Could it be Kalini?

He had to know, which was why he went looking for her. Had to find her. A connection existed between them. Forged during that kiss.

What did it mean?

Kalini might have resisted his charm, but others fell for it. He easily got a ride that dumped him near her truck. He stared at the house attached to the driveway. He already knew she lived on the second floor. She was up there right now despite his advice to flee.

She was so naïve. She'd walked into the jaws of danger because she wanted answers. But could he blame her? He'd also gone looking for his roots. He still wished he'd never bothered.

A part of him wanted to grab her and run. Shake her from this dangerous course she'd chosen.

However, he was weak. So very, very weak. He needed to feed first. Not the type of food for the belly, but his essence.

He lay in wait for his prey, who arrived not long after, talking on his phone. "I'm packing up now and will be on the road with the goods in an hour."

Only once his meal hung up did Urion make his presence known. "Hello, Ben."

## CHAPTER 11

DEAR DIARY: THAT SCREAM YOU HEARD?
ME, BECAUSE I WISHED I COULD TURN BACK
TIME AND SAY YES TO URION WHEN HE
ASKED ME TO GO WITH HIM.

Boy DID I feel dumb for not going with Urion. And why had I ditched him?

Because he made my panties wet. You'd think at my age, I'd know how to deal with it. Alas, I became a flustered woman. A horny woman, with no idea how to find the man at the root of my problem.

But I tried. In between making the brownies—that Ben never showed up for, so I ate them—I hopped onto the internet and searched for missing men named Urion. I also read the various news reports about the fire at CTI. Nothing jumped out. I didn't have a sudden revelation.

It didn't look good for my quest. I consoled myself with making a massive dinner. I made way more than I needed, theorizing it would make great leftovers. As the seven-layer lasagna and shepherd's pie baked, I showered and dressed in something other than a rag, arguing to myself that being unemployed and without any leads didn't mean I should be a slob.

As for the lip gloss? I put it on because a tiny part of me expected the knock at my door.

How? Call it intuition. It had been positively shivering all day long.

My dog, who'd only realized we had a visitor because of the knock, lifted his head, uttered one massive woof, and then went back to napping.

"Some guard dog you are," I huffed as I answered.

Urion stood in the frame, looking less unkempt than before. His hair was combed and clean. He wore a polo shirt, slacks that molded his legs, and loafers on his feet. His features still held a hint of gauntness, but his eyes were bright like in my dreams. His presence rolled over me and left me hyper aware.

"What are you doing here? How did you find me?"

"I followed my nose."

"More like probably got access to some employee files. Despite how movies portray it, stalking isn't cute or sexy." Lie. I was totally turned on. Here was to hoping he'd not come to murder me because I'd feel pretty dumb in a second.

"I needed to see you."

"What happened to you leaving town? I thought it was urgent."

"I'm not leaving without you," he declared, stepping inside, and finally my dog turned into a dog. He jumped off the couch and growled.

"Murphy!" I exclaimed.

Urion held out his hand. "He won't bite me. What an interesting mix. Where did you get him?"

"My parents found him for me." It was right after my place got broken into. They only stole my box of Captain Crunch and a jar of peanut butter, but my mom freaked. Insisted I needed a dog. Then proceeded to get me the laziest one out there. Murphy hated long walks. Loved to drive with his head out the window. And wouldn't eat canned dog food but loved Chef Boyardee in a can. Unheated. Just straight into his bowl.

Urion turned his hand flat, and my dog approached and shoved his head against it. "He's a special creature."

"Yup. The best, and another reason I can't just up and leave. Where I go, Murphy does, too."

"Then we'll bring him."

He kept speaking as if it were a foregone conclusion. But why me?

Instead I asked, "Hungry?" I headed for the kitchen to pull the food from the oven. Since I couldn't decide, he had two choices. A shepherd's pie. Ground beef roasted with garlic, caramelized onions and mushrooms with a thick layer of cream corn then fluffy mashed potatoes. The instant kind because I liked them better than the peeled and boiled variety.

The butter I'd melted turned the top golden crispy brown. The baguette I'd made was ready for tearing. I hefted the two-foot tray of casserole onto the stovetop, along with the lasagna. I wasn't sure if I wanted meat and potatoes or pasta, so I'd made both and had already uncorked a bottle of wine.

I gestured to a plate. "Help yourself." Because I wasn't serving him. Super hungry, I spooned a generous portion from each dish onto my plate and tore off eight inches of baguette. I cracked it open and slathered it with butter before swiping at my shepherd's pie, slopping it on, and bringing it to my mouth.

Food porn. I groaned. Mom was always making weird fancy shit as I was growing up. She never understood my love of the simple things, like the tang and salt of the meat layer with the sweetness of the corn blended with the creaminess of the potatoes.

I then alternated with the lasagna and its spicy Bolognese sauce and gooey cheese layers, plus one of pepperoni to give it a slight pizza feel.

"This is good." A grunted praise that had me looking over to see Urion sopping up the remains with a hunk of bread.

"I know. Have more," I graciously offered.

"I will, but first, take off that ridiculous binder."

"I don't know what you're talking about." I sucked back my wine and poured another.

"The thing you have confining your tail. Take it off or I will remove it for you."

Would he? He just might. I was tempted to let him. The wrestling might lead to fun times. Instead, I left the room and returned with my tail dipping boldly below my calf-length skirt.

He nodded in approval. "Better. At least until you learn to properly vanish it."

"Vanish? Sounds ominous." I slid back into my chair. My freed tail was able to slide to the side so my ass actually hit the seat.

"I would have called it self-preservation. Most of us learn young how to hide what we are."

"You keep saying 'we'?"

He slid a plate in front of me. "We have more in common than you might think."

While I was stripping, he'd ladled the rest of my pie, pasta, and bread out. We ate the whole thing, the conversation paused while we consumed.

Once done, it seemed natural to end up on the couch. Opposite ends with less than two feet between us. Too close. Too far.

He sighed. "We really should be moving. They could arrive at any time."

"Who's they?" I sipped my wine.

"The white coats who made us."

"Made us from what?" I asked, feeling mellow from the wine.

"In your case, I'd say mostly dragon."

## CHAPTER 12

AN UNREDACTED PORTION OF A MEDICAL FILE: A HIGHLY INTELLIGENT CREATURE, SUBJECT Z SHOWS REMARKABLE MENTAL ACUITY.

BEING smart didn't mean Urion understood people. He'd made assumptions about Kalini. How could she not know the basics about her origin?

The wine she spewed on him as she choked, "Dragon?" corrected his misassumption.

How could she not know? It seemed so obvious to him.

Still coughing, she ran for the kitchen, snaring some paper towels and returning to dab at the stain on his shirt. As if he cared. The shirt didn't belong to him. He'd have bought something more comfortable, but Ben's choice in attire limited him.

*Ah, Ben. If only your bosses had listened when you recommended terminating me.*

"Good thing the couch is covered in dark fabric, or I'd be losing my cleaning deposit." She moved from swiping ineffectually at his shirt to the sofa cushion.

"How did you not know you were part dragon?"

"Because dragons aren't real."

"They're real, just rare."

"And you think I'm one of them? Ha!" She stalked to her kitchen to dispose of the garbage and pour more wine.

"I don't think, I know you are."

"Fuck off," she spat. Her eyes flashed with anger. "How dare you mock me?"

"Mock you?" He tried to see how he'd offended her.

"You think it's funny to mess with me? I've had to live with being different my whole life. How dare you turn it into a joke?"

"I didn't say it to upset you." It had simply never occurred to him she hadn't figured it out. When she shifted, did she not look in a mirror? Even now, he could see the tip of her tail. A tail that didn't vanish. Odd.

"I'm not upset," was her tight reply. "I'm just finding your bullshit hard to believe."

"Surely you've wondered what you are." In his case, he'd always known. His early years with doctors and the testing he went through gave him a wealth of knowledge—and pain.

"I wondered and the conclusion was dinosaur," she said quickly before she took a sip of her wine.

It took him a second to digest. "You thought you were part dinosaur?" He couldn't help it; he laughed.

Her scowl went with her growled, "How am I

supposed to know what I am? It's not as if anyone has ever seen or heard of a baby with a tail hatching out of an egg." Her eyes widened as she blurted out, "Forget I said that."

"An egg would explain where you got the dragon gene from, given humans can't carry a hatchling to term."

"You seem to know a lot about dragons."

"I know a lot about many things." Seen things she couldn't imagine.

She blinked at him. Said nothing for a moment. Abruptly, she stood. "I want to show you something." She left and went into another room, only to immediately emerge with a cardboard container. "I call this the box of lies."

He arched a brow. "Dare I inquire what's inside?"

She slapped it onto the low table flanking the couch. "Growing up, I thought my parents only ever told me the truth. They never hid the fact I came from an egg or that I was created in a lab. I always knew there was something different about me and not just because of the tail. But they never said how I was made, or with what. Who. Ugh." She drank some more wine.

"Other than your obvious dragon nature, have you exhibited other characteristics?"

Her face went through a myriad of expressions before she said, "No."

"Are you sure?"

Her shoulders slumped. "Do you think I haven't wished I was special?"

"You are." He said it softly. Truthfully.

She stared at him, her cheeks turning pink. She ducked her head as she opened the box, revealing a stack of paper. Atop it, as if a weight to hold it, a brittle piece of eggshell, mauve in color.

She held it in her hand, lips turned slightly down. "I thought I was special. Unique. I don't know how many times I watched the video of my birth. They kept it, you know. Despite my mom being worried about the fact it existed, my dad refused to get rid of it. I thought it was because he loved me so much. But it was proof, proof it really happened." She spoke slowly, and he didn't interrupt. She unburdened herself, and he listened. "Mom and Dad were excited in the video. My mom thought I might be some sort of extinct exotic bird that would rival an ostrich." She snorted and rolled her shoulders. "Never did get those long legs."

"You have fine legs." They'd look great around his waist. The shocking thought almost had him missing her next words.

"There's pictures of us. Me just born, mom crying as she holds me. Even my dad beaming proudly. Always thought it was because they were so happy, but turns out, it was because they saw me as their ticket to fame and fortune. I was an experiment to them." The words emerged short and angry. "A study so they could document everything."

Some of the stapled sheaves of paper appeared medical in nature. But amongst them peeked yellowed newspaper clippings and pictures.

He grabbed the official sheets first. "Summarize for me. What do they say?"

"Size. Weight. What I ate. What I played. From the moment of my birth, everything I did was documented by my parents. Every single scrape I got. My rare fevers and colds. The quarterly blood tests. Tissue samples. I thought they did it to keep me healthy and safe."

"But?" he prodded.

She blinked back tears, and her voice tightened as she said, "While I get the impression they loved me, in the end, I was a science experiment. My mom and dad worked for the lab. They were assigned to watch over my egg. They knew their lab was experimenting, knew and condoned it. When protestors actually did storm the place, they stole my egg."

He could imagine what happened. "And you were born."

"Yup and they decided to keep me rather than hand me back because how else could they study and eventually claim credit for me?" The words emerged with bitter bite.

"They told you this?" he asked.

"Yes and no. They claimed in their letter that while I started out as a project for them, they fell in love with me the moment I was born. Said they did their best to keep me safe."

He could hear the anguish, and it hurt him. He'd learned a long time ago to not let people get close. However, she'd not grown up as he had, hiding, knowing better than to trust humans. To trust no one for that matter.

"If they planned to use you, wouldn't they have done it while you were still young?"

"I'm not old," she retorted hotly.

"Not for your kind, no; however I'm not sure how waiting benefitted them."

"Why does it matter?"

"Because it calls into question your interpretation of their actions." Urion couldn't have said why he wanted to ease her suffering over her parents. He didn't care.

She stared at him. "How dare you stick a pin in my righteous indignation." She slumped. "Guess it doesn't matter now because they died in a freak accident, and CTI burned to the ground. I'll never find out who my actual DNA donors were."

"Dragon, and some human." The tang proved distinct. But there was something else, too. He'd not been exaggerating when he'd compared her to a summer storm, the kind that electrified the air with ozone.

"How can you tell? And before you answer, know

that I've compared my blood against thousands of profiles. Animal. Human. Even bug."

"I can smell it, and so could you if you tried."

Her nose wrinkled. "I'd rather not go around sniffing people. It's weird."

"How is it weird? You use your eyes to see. Your hands to feel. Why not your nose to smell out what those senses might not detect?"

"I'm not a dog."

"No, but you are a dragon hybrid."

"Am I really?" A wistful note entered the query. "I always kind of thought it was more dinosaur than anything."

The very idea had him snorting. "Scientists long ago realized the dinosaurs had nothing more to offer than a plodding size. Hence why they began seeking out more gifted subjects."

"Like dragons. Yay for me. Now, if only I could belch fire." She tipped her wine down her throat.

"You probably can do more than you realize. I had no idea the depths of my own abilities until they were tested by the white coats."

"Have you spent your entire life locked up?"

"No, but I have been in their grasp for a large portion of it." He shook his head. "I was born in their custody and only got away from the doctors in my teens. It happened during a mass revolt that saw a bunch of us fleeing a hidden compound. I've been living underground since then until my capture."

She stared at him. "Fuck." Eloquently spoken and heartfelt.

"Yes, fuck. But on the other hand, I managed to stay out of human clutches for more than a decade."

"Out of how many years?"

He actually wasn't sure of his exact age, so he shrugged. "Too many. So trust me when I say your parents might have lied to spare your feelings, but it sure beat living in a cage and being treated like a rat. You have no idea what it's like to be born in captivity. I never had a mother or a father. No birthday cakes or toys. Just an endless stream of whitecoats and guards and tests. The first time I was in their custody, I was given some mobility. The second, they kept me deeply drugged."

"That sucks."

Her vehement exclamation had him smiling wryly. "It does, and it's what you have to look forward to when they catch you."

"I won't get caught."

"That's what I thought, and I turned out to be wrong. It's why you and I will always have to hide."

"I'm not hiding."

He snorted.

She tried to argue. "I have a job. I go out."

"For now, but you live in fear that you might be discovered."

"They'll think I'm some weird medical freak."

He uttered a bark that wasn't quite laughter. "Now

who's talking crazy? You're deluded if you think you'll get off so easily."

"It's not fair." Her lower lip jutted temptingly. "I didn't ask for this. And neither did you."

"Fairness has nothing to do with it."

"Then why is this happening? What's the point of playing God?"

"Because the whitecoats can. They've been given the means to experiment without repercussion. It's why we need to stay away from them." Urion had a feeling the next time they caught him he'd be taken apart so they could study the parts they liked. If they ever found out about Kalini, they'd use her, too.

With her head tilted and hair falling to the side, he noticed a hint of an out-dent on her forehead. As if nubs pushed against skin. "How long since your last full shift?" he asked. He knew shifters had to do it on a regular basis or else the pressure would start manifesting. Was that why she had a tail?

She stared at him with utter incomprehension. "Shift as in a car? My truck's an automatic."

The reply creased his brow. "What do you call it then, morphed? Changed shape?"

She shook her head. "I'm not a werewolf or weredino. This is who I am." The claim held a combative note.

"You've always had a tail." Stated, not asked.

The downturned lips spoke of her displeasure. "I thought I already told you. I was born with it."

Born with was often related to a stress thing. Most people didn't have the control needed to just shift parts of their body. It usually took a strong emotion to sustain a half shift, such as being born. Once someone calmed down, it went away. Hers apparently didn't.

"Have you ever tried to change your appearance? To wish away the tail or have the rest of you match it?"

"That's impossible."

"Is it?" He held out his hand and concentrated on it, drawing from the times he'd practiced— mostly inspired by mutant movies—to fully use his abilities.

Kalini gasped as the darkest of scales covered the flesh, matte black with a deep blue under sheen. His fingers thickened, and the claws poking from the tips were ebony and wicked sharp.

"What are you doing? How?" She stared at him, not afraid, he was happy to see, but intrigued.

"A shifter can change its body between species."

A frown knit her brow. "Is that what I'm called? My parents called me a hybrid."

"Which is the name scientists give those they mix that usually wouldn't occur in nature."

"Oh." For some reason, she appeared both angry and sad at once.

It bothered him which might be why he said, "Personally, I prefer the more popular term, Misfit. It's what they call those of us who don't fit anywhere. Supposedly there's even a sanctuary out there for us run by an ex-stripper." What he didn't mention was sccording to the urban legend, its pole-loving queen was a mix of angel and demon, built in a lab. If rumor were true, she'd sent out an invitation to all the Misfits who needed a home to join her.

It was tempting. It would be nice to have a place where he didn't have to watch himself constantly.

Limbo, though, sounded too good to be true. What if seeking it out caused him to reveal himself and launched a trap? Not that he worried too much about it because he had no idea how to get there.

"Me, a misfit?" She clung to the word.

"A dragon misfit." Which was more acceptable than his mixture.

She snorted. "That makes it sound cooler than I am. Maybe other hybrids or misfits can do this shifting thing. Me? I don't turn into some majestic beast who can fly or a sexy seductress with a nice ass."

"Are you sure?"

"Don't you think I wish I were a dragon?"

"You are. Your scent doesn't lie." He'd met a fair number of dragons by accident. Almost died because he'd apparently encroached on some firedrake's territory. But when the mighty Murtaugh realized Urion's blood was far from pure, he did something worse than kill Urion.

Murtaugh mocked him.

Urion got mad, and in the end, Murtaugh the one-eye apologized by giving Urion a lifetime pass through his territory.

"You keep talking about smell. Well, if you're weird like me, how come all I smell is cologne?"

"What kind?" he asked, leaning forward. Did she realize she'd come closer to sniff him?

Her head tilted as she inhaled and said, "Like nutmeg and honeyed milk."

"Really?"

"Yes." She eyed him. "What's it called?"

"Me."

## CHAPTER 13

FROM THE NOTES OF THE PSYCHIATRIST ASSIGNED TO SUBJECT Z: …WHILE NOT YET A TEENAGER, SIGNS OF ARROGANCE ARE MANIFESTING.

AT HIS REPLY, Kalini blinked. "What do you mean?"

"You asked about my cologne. I'm not wearing any." He grinned.

"Then it's your soap." She tried to find an excuse.

"I've not had a proper shower since they caught me." Which made him long for some soap to scrub away their touch. He knew what kind of samples they'd bled and milked him for.

"Well, good for you, even when you stink, you smell good."

"Thanks, I think." His lips twitched. She was a foot shorter than him with an arrogant attitude. Her skewed bangs didn't detract from her fierce cuteness. Even more attractive, she wasn't impressed by him at all. "Since I'm pretty sure you want to change topics, let's go back to shifting. The tail is obviously in place. What about claws?"

She held out her hands. "In need of a manicure but not gnarly."

"Feet?"

"I'm able to wear open-toe sandals if that helps."

"Horns?"

She pressed her lips before shaking her head.

"Don't lie. I can see their outline. Have they ever come out?"

She shrugged. "Not that I've noticed."

"Wings?"

"No."

"Are you sure?"

"Would you like me to strip so you can look?" she snapped.

"As a matter of fact, I'd love to see you naked," he drawled.

"Not happening," she lied. He caught it only because her heat trended upwards.

"You're the one who offered."

"It's called sarcasm."

"Actually, I would have said deflection. We both know you'd like to get naked for me."

"Would not," she huffed. "And you're really starting to piss me off."

"Angry enough to shift?" He tried to catch her off guard.

"Because I can do it, just like that?" She clicked her fingers.

"You obviously need to practice. Think of it as a

muscle. You never learned how to use it, and it's going to take practice to exercise it and manipulate it like it's meant."

"I thought shapeshifting only happened during full moons."

"The urge can be stronger, mostly because the lunar light ignites usually dormant pheromones in the atmosphere that affect certain species."

"Moon madness is real. Cool. Maybe I should dance naked in its light one night."

He heard her sarcasm, but he answered with all seriousness. "You should definitely try it. Very liberating. But the next one isn't for two weeks, and you should start learning how to control it now."

"I don't know what you mean by control."

"I think you do, but you're scared to try." He deliberately goaded her. Heightened emotions would make it more likely to happen.

"Try to what? Wish my tail gone? Don't you think I've wished it away?" She huffed in hot irritation.

"It won't ever fully go away. It's a part of you."

"It's a hunk of dead meat." She deliberately leaned over and grabbed it, heaving it. It hung in her grip. "It doesn't do anything.

"It doesn't move at all?"

She shook her head. "Never has. I don't feel it either. It's the reason I can contort and hide it."

"You have to feel something." He reached out to touch the warm scales. Ran his finger down it, and she didn't react. The tail didn't either. It should have whipped away, slapped him for the nerve of touching.

He poked her. "This?"

A popped, "Nope."

It seemed impossible. "If it's been dead your entire life, why keep it?" he asked. He wondered at the logic of it. A paralyzed limb that served no purpose?

She dropped her tail, and did her best to tuck it out of sight. "Because my parents told me it made me special."

"You are special."

She uttered a sound. "And according to you, I'm going to probably end up in some lab used in experiments."

"I can help you stay out of their grasp."

"Says the guy who's been their guest for how many years?"

He scowled. "I made a mistake. It won't happen again."

"And why should I listen to anything you say? After all, I've made it more than three decades without getting caught."

"Eventually your luck will run out."

"Why would you want to help me? Shouldn't you be hightailing it as far as you can from here?"

How to explain he felt compelled to help her? She'd asked before why he'd sought her out. He simply had no choice. He was meant to be by her side. As terrifying as it sounded.

"I don't want to see you get hurt."

"Why?" she asked. "We've only barely met."

"I want to get to know you."

"Which sounds great until I wonder if you're a psycho serial killer."

"If I were, I would have killed you by now."

"Maybe you're toying with me?" She arched a brow.

He smiled. "Do I look like the type who would tease you mercilessly?" He purred it and her lips parted.

"I think you're dangerous."

"You'd be right. Shift."

"What?" She exhaled in startlement.

"Show me who you truly are, or I am going to kiss you." There was more than one kind of strong emotion, and since he found himself loath to make her sad or angry with him, that left a more pleasurable option.

Her eyes widened. "You aren't kissing me."

"Shift or move that tail and I won't."

"I can't."

"Then I'm kissing you."

"I'm saying no." Said and yet she didn't move as he advanced on her. Her pupils dilated, her lips parted, her heart raced.

Did she, like him, remember their last kiss? On that other plane of consciousness. It had struck him as electric. He wanted to claim it affected him deeply because it had been too long. That would be a lie. He'd gone long stints where he'd abstained before.

Never.

Ever.

Had he desired someone so ardently to the point he stood in her space, staring down at her, willing her to stop the madness possessing him.

To kiss him and put him out of his misery.

"Maybe you've been asleep too long and don't know that when a woman says no, it means no."

He leaned down. "Are you going to really try and make me believe you don't want me to kiss you?"

"Are you going to be a bully about it?"

Would he force the issue?

"No." Damn her. He took a step back.

Her gaze narrowed. "What game are you playing?"

Rather than lie, he said, "I was trying to see if I could trigger you."

"By pissing me off?"

"Actually, I was going for seduction. Sexual energy is quite powerful."

She laughed. Hard and bitter. "Did you just assume the girl with a tail never got laid? I've got information for you, honey. I've had sex. I've had orgasms, and while nice, I didn't suddenly sprout horns or breathe fire."

Despite not being chaste himself, a fierce jealousy filled him. She'd been with another. She had a comparison. What if he paled?

What if his self-doubt shut the fuck up?

"Those men weren't me." He knew without a doubt their coupling would be explosive.

"Are you trying to goad me into kissing you?"

"I don't know what I'm doing." The honest truth.

## CHAPTER 14

DEAR DIARY: APPARENTLY, I WANT TO BE
SINGLE. FOREVER.

Why was I fighting so hard? I wanted Urion to kiss me. Kiss me and take me right there. On that wall. Tits out. Tail up.

Why couldn't I throw the guy a bone? Or at least play with his? He admitted he didn't know what he was doing. A statement that hit me as vulnerable and adorable. Probably one of the sexist things a guy ever said to me, too, if one discounts the usually drunken and slurred, "You look hot. Wanna fuck?" I understood Urion might still turn out to be a psycho serial killer, but on the flip side, he was a possibly murdering monster interested in me.

Yeah, me. It made me want to strut. It definitely had me aching for another kiss.

Only the jerk stepped away. Despite his teasing threat, he wouldn't force me. Didn't he realize I wanted him to push me against the wall and kiss me? I wanted someone, overcome by passion, to seduce me.

Wanted it more than anything.

But he just had to be a nice guy and respect me.

Fuck that. I shouldn't have said no, and as a woman, I reserved the right to change my mind.

I stepped into him and pressed my mouth to his.

He inhaled sharply, surprised. Would he reject me?

A part of me feared it, which might be why I kept my eyes open. I wanted to see if he recoiled.

Instead, he wrapped his arms around me, and with him staring back, I had the most intense kiss. The intimacy of it, the fact we had our gazes locked. I had no doubt he was sober. He saw me clearly. Still wanted me.

Hottest thing ever, according to my wet panties.

He rumbled a noise against my lips, and I got my wish. My back hit the wall, and he ground into me.

I might have had a mini 'gasm. I certainly appeared to have entered a sensual heaven. It was passionate. Thrilling. Hot. Embracing him engaged all of my senses. It had me writhing wantonly, and through it all, he stared at me.

Connected with something deep inside.

I wanted more, and he read my mind. My skirt dragged up at his tugging. My wanton self spread her legs. Needed his touch.

He stroked his hand up my thigh, humming in enjoyment as he slid his tongue over and under mine.

I trembled. Had another mini climax. I clenched so hard it almost hurt. I wanted him inside me.

His hand slid between my thighs and stroked over my panties. I broke our stare as my head went back and I moaned.

"Fuck me, you're wet," he murmured.

"Just a little," I gasped. Still a smartass.

He dropped to his knees in front of me, his hands on my thighs.

"What are you doing?"

"Making you come," he purred against my mound, the hotness of his breath making my toes curl.

Yes, please. I'd never had someone go down on me before, but I'd fantasized about it.

Wanted to know how it felt.

Hips tilting proved the only invitation he required. His mouth grabbed hold of me, and I cried out.

Oh my god. It felt so fucking good. He played with me. Teasing me through the fabric and I shuddered. Shivered. Thrust my hips against him. Forget having any semblance of control.

My panties were shifted aside, and he blew on me. I almost came again. I squeezed tight and whimpered.

"How can I resist you when you smell and taste so good?" he murmured against me before licking me. Down there. A wet swipe that had me bucking. He held me firm, his hands on my thighs, his face between them. He licked me and tickled my clit.

I cried out. Moaned. Pushed against him. Was

already about to come when he thrust his fingers into me.

Holy climax. I came hard. I squeezed harder. I am pretty sure I left my body for a moment, and when I returned, it was going through waves of bliss.

That was a real orgasm. The kind to steal your breath. Take your voice. Leave every limb languorous. He stood with a cocky grin, a soft gaze, and a hard-on poking me in the belly. I could feel it, larger than before.

Making me come turned him on.

He kissed me, and it was strange tasting myself on his lips. We were back to staring at each other, and despite my orgasm, I felt a quiver. He touched me, and that quiver trebled.

We weren't done. He fingered me, and I moaned into his mouth.

Could I come again? Would it kill me? I wanted to find out. I reached for him, boldly grabbing him, and he sucked in a breath. His eyes widened before shuttering, half lidded.

He pulsed in my grip. Now I held the power. I tugged at him, and his hips moved with me. Steel wrapped in velvety skin. I brought a leg around his hips to open myself to him and rubbed the tip of his hard shaft against me.

My turn to gasp, and I saw the passion smoldering in his stare.

I wanted him inside me. Wanted to come on him. Feel him come inside me.

He growled. "What is it about you that makes me unable to resist?"

I could have asked the same. I sucked his tongue and began to guide him into me, wondering, given the size of him, if he'd fit.

Apparently, I wasn't going to find out because my dog chose that moment to cock block me.

Murphy growled. A deep, rumbly sound, and Urion immediately halted the progress of his dick.

I could have cried. His head turned as he chose to watch my dog, rising from his nap on the floor. Murphy padded to the door, sniffing at the crack under it before turning to eye me. Wait, he was eyeing Urion.

Was Murphy telling the guy about to make me see heaven for a second time to leave? The nerve!

"Ignore my dog." I tried to get Urion's focus back on me.

"He heard something."

"Yeah, the sound of my door closing so we can have some privacy," I muttered.

"Shh."

The guy, who'd a minute ago been slurping and making me see stars, shh-ed me. Well that was fun. I dragged my skirt down as he tucked himself away.

Sob.

He took a step toward Murphy and dropped to one knee beside him. Just a few seconds and then I swear the guy offered my dog a nod before saying, "Good job." And to me, "We have to go."

"Why?"

"Because we are about to have company, and we don't have time to argue about it," he bit out, the passionate guy replaced by the arrogant and demanding version.

"I beg to differ. I am not taking off with you just because Murphy heard something outside." Although, it should be noted, my dog only rarely, and I mean rarely, ever said *woof*.

"You're wasting time. They'll be here any moment."

"Who?"

"People who don't mean either of us well."

I glared at him. "And whose fault is that? If I'm on their radar, it's your fault."

"Possibly. Deal with it." He didn't deny or apologize. He glared at the door. "Dammit. They're here. Is there another way out? We can't use your main door."

"That's it unless you're flying."

"We're not high enough for that. Best we could hope for is a glide. Can you climb?"

"Maybe. But I know my dog can't."

"Don't worry about your dog. He's got the best odds out of the three of us."

"I am not leaving my dog behind." I remained firm on that point.

It was then I heard it. The thump of several car

doors outside. Still didn't mean anything. Could be people going to visit my downstairs neighbor.

Urion tensed. "We have to go now, Kalini."

Out through a window? But what about Murphy?

*Bang. Bang. Bang.*

I smiled in triumph, as the knocking wasn't on my level. "Ha. Guess you were wrong."

The last smartass thing I said a second before the window in the kitchen broke and an object, pouring smoke, sailed in.

## CHAPTER 15

DEAR DIARY: THE SEX WAS STILL WORTH THE TROUBLE.

SMOKE POURED INTO MY APARTMENT. I might have stared stupidly at it until I passed out if Urion hadn't tossed me over his shoulder.

"Put me down!" A halfhearted demand that he ignored as he sprinted for my bedroom and slammed the door shut. I almost protested, "What about Murphy?" only to realize the dog had made it inside first. Faster than he looked.

"We need to get out of here. That smoke is meant to put us to sleep."

Well, that explained why I was teetering on my feet, in the mood for a nap. "Stop with the 'us' thing. They're after you." He was the fugitive. Not me.

No one knew my secret, meaning I was safe.

I hoped. At the same time, who waited outside? Could it be that the authorities had arrived to take my dangerous guest into custody? Or would it be the men in the white coats?

Either way, would I let them take the only person who might truly understand me? The one man who saw me and didn't turn from me in disgust?

Rather than reply, he glanced out the window. I could have told him not to bother. On this side of the apartment, there wasn't even a tree to break our fall.

Urion dragged the window open, the vinyl sash fairly quiet. He glanced down. Straight drop.

*Pfft.*

The strange noise had me blinking and wondering just how fast Urion moved because one second he framed the window, and the next, he hit the floor.

"Get down," he snapped. "They've already surrounded the place."

I noticed the thing sticking in my wall. "Is that a dart? Are they shooting at us?"

"Yup. Try to not get hit."

"What did you drag me into?" I squeaked in alarm as I hit the floor.

"This is the danger of being a misfit in a human world."

"Or is the peril in knowing you?"

"You wouldn't have avoided this forever. Think of it this way, though, at least you have me to help get us out of this."

"How do you plan to do that?" I gestured to the smoke seeping under the door. "We are stuck in here."

"Don't worry. I have a plan." The man turned a

cocky grin on me and winked. Then he glanced to my dog. "Cover us."

"We are not using my dog as a shield," I protested, only to have my jaw drop as my dog ran for the window and leaped. Murphy soared through that gap, and I expected to hear a thump and a yelp.

There was nothing to indicate my dog got hurt, but those outside went wild. I heard the sound of more missiles being fired.

Then a loud "*Grawr.*"

My baby. My Murphy. I tried not to wince as his snarl was met with a scream. Their fault for shooting at my poor puppy.

Urion stood and gestured. "Let's go while he's distracting them."

"Out the window? It's like a ten- to twelve-foot drop."

"Thirteen actually. Let's go." He snapped his fingers.

I hesitated, only to hear a loud bang as something slammed against my apartment door. The door handle rattled. I ran for the window, glanced out, and hesitated. It was far.

Before I could tell Urion he needed to rethink his plan, he grabbed me and dove through. I thanked the Lord, and Jesus Christ, that the window proved to be of the wide variety, or he'd have scraped me off like gum on a shoe.

My scream got caught as we plummeted, the night

air cold against my flushed cheeks. I expected to splat, only somehow, Urion hit the ground, knees bent. He kept me from smashing. I expected to hear him cry out or at the least stumble, but the man landed like a cat, and the moment he had me steadied on my two feet, he grabbed my hand and dragged me. No one was shooting at us, but I could hear yells. A glance back and up at my window showed someone leaning out of it, aiming a weapon, his face covered by a gas mask.

Urion yanked me to the side, pulling me out of the path of a flying dart. He then had us bolting past my dog, who stood over a prone body.

Shit, had Murphy killed someone? I'd get him the best lawyer. Claim it was self-defense in doggie court.

My hysterical mind tried to find a distraction from the madness.

Urion appeared to be aiming for the street when another car slammed to a screaming stop and people piled out. With guns!

"Hands up or we'll shoot," shouted some guy who sounded as if he'd enjoy pulling that trigger.

I heeded their demand. Hands over my head, looking as benign as possible. "Don't shoot me. I haven't done anything."

"Seriously?" Urion muttered.

"He's taken a civilian hostage," the gruff man shouted. "Lock down the area."

"On it, sir," someone snapped and ran off from the foursome advancing.

This group wasn't wearing gas masks, but they did have on black uniforms, military style with no insignia. Police? Government agency?

Didn't matter. We were screwed. I was all too conscious of my untucked tail. They hadn't noticed it yet, but given they beckoned me closer, the streetlight would soon make it clear.

I didn't dare move. I couldn't help but recall what Urion said. How he'd been a prisoner. Would I even rate that level of treatment with only a tail?

Two of the soldier dudes moved closer, holding out zip ties, while the other two were joined by more guys in gas masks, all armed. Bad odds.

Urion said nothing, although he appeared grim. I wondered if he regretted wasting his escape window giving me an orgasm. I certainly wished we'd gotten down to business sooner. Because we'd obviously never get another chance.

"I'm sorry," I muttered.

"You should have listened when I first said we had to go. Don't blame me for what happens next," was his soft reply.

As I turned to admonish him hotly, the guy in charge barked, "Don't move or we will shoot."

I froze, but my dog? The laziest mutt inexistence chose that moment to stand between me and the guys with guns.

In their defense, a small-pony-sized dog, growling

with hackles up, must have seemed scary. But that gave them no right to shoot at my dog!

"Murphy!" I yelled upon seeing the darts sticking out of his body. Anger coursed through me, hot and quick.

And then I saw nothing. A sudden zap filled the air, and in the blink of an eye, all the power in the neighborhood went out.

## CHAPTER 16

DEAR DIARY: OUR GOVERNMENT REALLY
NEEDS TO UPGRADE THE POWER GRID.

THE SUDDEN DARKNESS caused everyone to freeze, but it didn't last. I could see the soldiers standing there stupidly, and then one of them was down as my dog pounced with a snarl.

The act set off a chain reaction. Guns fired. Men screamed. A woman, too, judging by the higher pitch. In the chaos that followed, Urion grabbed hold of my hand and dragged me toward the fence to the neighbor's yard. He practically tossed me over it before joining me in a leap that made me wonder if the man had wings on his feet. I didn't see any, but then again, I'd been blind to not realize I wasn't the only hybrid alive.

I even had a name. Misfit.

A dragon misfit

The idea intrigued, but reality took precedence. I'd no sooner landed and stumbled than I whirled. "Murphy!"

I wasn't about to leave him behind, only I realized he was suddenly there, making me wonder how he managed to make the jump over the fence. Didn't matter. I quickly plucked the two darts sticking out of his fur and dropped them to the ground. Lucky for me, they'd not given him a large dose of whatever sleeping agent was inside.

I wanted to hug my pup, but he trotted away, heading for the next fence. With Urion tossing me, we moved away from the yelling. Stayed away from the windows with candles and curious faces peering outward. We avoided the yards where cigarette smokers and the curious emerged to wonder, "What happened to the power?"

After a while we slowed our pace. We could no longer hear those who'd come to arrest us, and I needed a break. I collapsed on a wicker chair, part of a set sitting on patio stones laid in a square.

My dog, who could apparently also leap fences in a single bound—yet could barely go three feet in the winter to pee—flopped on the grass. I just hoped it was a Murphy nap and not the drugs putting him to sleep.

Urion said nothing to me but cocked his head as if he listened. He probably did. I listened too, but heard nothing.

"Do you think we've lost them?" I asked.

He nodded. "It's too dark for them to see."

I didn't quite agree given I could see perfectly fine. "What now?" Because it occurred to me how screwed I was. My wallet. My phone. My truck. We'd left everything behind. Exactly what did Urion plan to do? Actually, fuck Urion. What did I plan to do?

"We need to get somewhere safe."

"And how do you plan to do that? We have nothing." I slapped my hands on my body. "No money. No wheels. Not even a change of underwear." Which I could have totally used.

"It's not safe to go back."

"And whose fault is that?" I snapped, only to feel contrite. He never asked for any of this. "Sorry. I'm a tad overwhelmed." My brain was too fried to work on a solution.

"We really should go. I don't know how wide of a net they can cast."

"Go where?" I asked a little hysterically. "Everything I have is back there." I pointed in what I thought was the direction of my apartment. With all my stuff. Mementos of my life. The ugly landscape I painted when I went through a Bob Ross phase, which my dad had displayed proudly in his home office. The locket my mom gave me after I virtually won the state spelling bee. My mom knew I'd win if I ever entered, but she worried about the undue focus on me. Her love for me led to her being overprotective. I might have started out as a science project, but deep down, I knew I became more than that to them.

I'd already lost my parents. I couldn't lose my only memories of them, too.

"I'm sorry, Kalini. We can't go back."

"But my stuff. I—" He suddenly moved close and hugged me to him, his body tense. I shut my mouth, and when he held up a finger, I glanced overhead. I saw nothing, yet I shivered.

I heard a whoosh before I saw the flames that suddenly rose in the night sky.

Want to bet my apartment was on fire? And I knew who to blame.

I whirled and hit Urion, yelling, "This is your fault."

## CHAPTER 17

SUBJECT Z SHOWS A RESISTANCE TO FIRE IN ONLY ONE OF HIS SHAPES. A GOOD THING HIS HEALING ABILITIES WORK IN EITHER FORM.

Urion let Kalini hit him. She'd earned the right to her anger because it was true. His enemies, now her enemies, had firebombed her home. They'd come to her home looking for him. His own fault for not questioning Ben before killing him. He should have asked if they knew about Kalini.

A sloppy mistake. He'd been making so many since he met her. He should have fled with her when he had a chance. Instead, she sat on the ground laughing, and then suddenly she was crying.

Ah shit.

He dropped to her side. "What's wrong?" He'd not sensed any injuries.

"Wh-wh-at's wr-wrong?" she sobbed. "Everything is wrong. I lost everything."

"Only material things."

"They were *my* things."

"I'm sorry. I never meant for any of this to happen." Never expected he'd find someone like her.

She sniffled. "I'm sorry, too. I shouldn't have gotten mad at you. It's not your fault some assholes are chasing you. Whatever happened to due process?"

"The people after us don't abide by any laws. It's what makes them so dangerous."

"I guess it could be worse. At least Murphy is okay." She eyed her dog flopped on the grass.

Did she realize what she'd adopted as a pet? He couldn't tell all the breeds that went into making Murphy, but he did know one for sure. Hell hound. The most dangerous canine in existence. They'd had a kennel with a pair when he was growing up in custody.

Dangerous fuckers. The doctors ended up having to put them down because they couldn't keep them contained, and when they got loose, blood ran in the halls. And there she was, scratching it behind the ears crooning, "Who's the most agile doggie in the whole wide world? You are." She snuggled it, and the dog bore it without eating her face.

Impressive.

Her tailed peeked from her skirt. A limp noodle that made him wonder with all that heightened emotion if she'd felt anything. Could she have had something to do with the sudden power glitch? It had been rather opportune.

Before he could ask, someone with a flashlight opened a sliding door to yell, "Get out of my yard!"

Urion grabbed Kalini's hand, and they fled, Murphy leading the way to the street.

"I can't believe we're abandoning my truck."

It was a shame. The vehicle had the size and luxury level to travel in comfort. "We'll get a new one."

"How? Neither of us has a wallet." The sirens came from the opposite end of the street, and she partially turned to see them arrive. They screamed to a stop, spilling firemen who would attempt in vain to put out the fire. He could have told them not to bother. Someone was wiping their tracks.

"I can't believe this is happening," she muttered. The light overhead stuttered. Glitching.

She didn't seem to notice as she trembled. He wrapped his fingers around hers and tugged her away.

She followed as if reluctantly, heaving a deep breath as she said, "Now what?"

"We look for a place to hide and figure out our next move."

"Isn't hiding the next move?"

He snorted. "Hiding is a fact of life. Our next move should be helping us to make that easier."

"Easier would be not having a tail," she huffed. "Do you know how long it takes me to make those special underpants?"

"What if we could find a way to not need anything at all?"

"Still saying no to amputation."

He shuddered. "Like fuck are we cutting it off.

Obviously, something is broken. We need to figure out why and fix it."

"Just like that?"

"You said before you wanted to know who you are."

"I thought I was a dragon."

"You are. But a broken one."

And once more, he uttered the wrong thing. She went rigid, yanked her hand from his.

"What's wrong?" he asked.

"Here I thought you actually liked me as I am."

"I do. Did I not prove that earlier?"

As they entered an area where the electricity worked, the streetlamps illuminated her pink cheeks. "Maybe you were faking it to get me to trust you."

"You need to stop imagining the worst. I have no issue with your tail, but it sounds like you do."

She started to say, "No, I don't," only to slump. "Guess I do. And this talk about doing something about it freaks me out. I'm a freak. A thing created in a lab. Maybe broken is the only thing I'll ever be."

Rather than offer a trite reply, he gave her something private that he'd never admitted to anyone else. "All my life I've known I was different. Treated like I had no feelings. When I escaped, I had this fantasy that everything would change. That others would see me for who I am. But humanity still struggles with those that are different. That don't conform. I soon realized that not only was I doomed to run and hide my whole life but that I'd be alone."

For a moment she didn't say anything, and he wanted to punch himself for being the sappiest fucker alive. How could he spill his inner secret? She'd think him weak.

She squeezed his hand. "I know that feeling."

And that was all they said as they walked out of the neighborhood onto a main street with a gas station and corner store. He left her on the corner and walked over alone. Judging his pace based on that of the guy coming out of the store. A glance in the window showed no one there but the clerk. As he walked in, his features changed, as did his hands.

When he gruffly said, "Give money." The pierced cashier behind the plastic shield smirked and said, "Like fuck. Your Halloween mask doesn't scare me."

Apparently, the clerk felt safe in his plastic cubicle.

Urion dug talons into it, piercing it easily, and tore it free.

That got some attention.

The cashier stammered, "I'll give it to you. Just give me a second." He slammed open the register and handed over a few fives, a twenty, and a ten. Pitiful.

He glared. "Really?"

The cashier shrugged, their slouchy neon hat holding a side part in place over one eye. "Since the pandemic most people pay with cards." He pointed to illuminated pad on the counter that read, Contactless payment.

What pandemic? How much had the world changed since he'd been captured? If this issue was widespread, he'd have to hit an ATM machine.

He emerged with the cash, not changing his face until he'd crossed the parking lot. He'd half expected Kalini to leave with her dog. Instead he found her hugging herself.

As soon as he got near, she said softly, "You robbed that store."

"Yup."

"Won't that make things worse for us?"

"We needed money."

"I have money in the bank."

"We can't touch that. They'll find you if you try."

Her lips pressed tight. "I can't just walk away from my life."

"If you try to go back, you'll be taken into custody and locked in a cell."

"And what are you suggesting? That we turn into Bonnie and Clyde and rob our way across America until we're caught or shot?"

"Do you have a better idea? Don't you think I wish we had a safe place to go?" A safe haven where they wouldn't have to hide.

"What about that Limbo place you mentioned before?"

"Sounds great but I don't know how to get there."

Not to mention, what if the rumors he heard weren't true? Everyone who played the telephone game knew how the truth could change.

"Given Limbo is a place for lost souls, then death is probably the only option." Her nose wrinkled. "Going on the record right now as saying I'm not ready for that."

"We are not dying."

She snorted. "Well, if you say so, then I guess we won't."

He glanced around. "We should get off the street. We're too visible."

"Where do you suggest we go? Our options are limited."

He glanced to the sky as if it would have an answer. He didn't know this city. He'd been asleep for years. He didn't even know who the president was. But he did know how the underground worked, a hidden ecosystem that existed under the human nose, mostly ignored so long as they didn't cause trouble.

"Do you know where the bad part of town is?" he asked.

"Not really. I've only been here a few days. Why? You looking to score some drugs or weapons?"

That brought a cough of laughter. "Not exactly. Information."

"About? Are you thinking we should be finding this Limbo?"

"I doubt such a place exists." Even if it did, would they want him? He'd done some bad things.

"Then what?"

He didn't want to tell her the strange thought that came to him. It had occurred to him that if Kalini's egg had been stolen, then was it possible the female that laid it was alive? Even if she wasn't, what if Kalini had family or could make a connection with other dragons? They might be able to help her with the tail and provide a safe haven.

He didn't want to get her hopes up, so instead of a reply, he asked, "Will you trust me?"

## CHAPTER 18

DEAR DIARY: I'M PUTTING MY FAITH IN A MAN WHO LITERALLY ESCAPED A BASEMENT A FEW DAYS AGO. I'VE NEVER FELT MORE ALIVE.

EYEING URION'S SERIOUS FACE, the right answer wouldn't come out. Trust him? I barely knew him.

Yet my lips moved. "Okay," I agreed. What could I blame my insanity on? Maybe I wasn't getting the right vitamins? Could it be that, despite my orgasm, all my blood remained in my groin? Very possible. I kept eyeing Urion as if he were a piece of steak and I wanted to eat him.

The more time I spent with him, the more overwhelming the urge. It helped we were busy walking with me complaining because we'd escaped without shoes. It didn't seem to bother Urion, who had massive feet. Mine, on the other hand, were much daintier. Soft. A size seven. I never had a problem finding a shoe in my size, which explained my collection. When I moved, I only brought two dozen with me. I donated the rest because I ran out of space. Two dozen shoes to none.

"I'm going to slice my foot open on something dirty and get a massive infection," I complained as I dodged a stone on the sidewalk.

"You'll be fine."

"Says you."

"Yes, says me. With your genes, I'll wager you heal faster than is normal. You're probably also crazy healthy."

"I do heal well." It never failed to amaze my parents when I scraped a knee or elbow and was fine the next day. "But I'll have you know I got sick as a kid." Flus, colds, tonsillitis. None lasted long, however.

"Our human skin is susceptible to virus, but you can avoid it by shifting."

There he went talking about shifting again. Maybe he could control it. After all he'd shown me how he could change his hand, his arm, but I wasn't the same as him. I did have to ask, "How does shifting help?"

"Human viruses don't flourish in other species. Shifting kills the microbe, so when they go back to their other skin, they're fine."

"Really?" Now that sounded useful. Shame I couldn't do it. "Ouch." My sole hit something small but sharp. Such a tough dragon. Not. You'd think with all the needles I'd been given in my life I wouldn't be such a wuss.

"Give me a second. I need to grab something." Once more Urion left me on the sidewalk and jaywalked across the street.

I dug my fingers into Murphy's fur. "Sorry for all the commotion."

*Yawn.* My dog lay down at my feet. All this walking had tired him out.

Urion headed up the porch steps of a house already dark for the night, unlike others on the street. Last time I'd checked a clock, it was after nine. How long had we been wandering?

I held my breath at the sudden sound of breaking glass. Urion had his hand through the pane of the front door. He unlocked and entered.

Oh shit. What was he doing? Should I run away before someone called the cops? Stay?

I hadn't decided as he emerged holding some slip-on shoes in his hand.

"You robbed that house!" I hissed as he returned.

"Yup."

"Hard to hide if you're leaving a trail of robberies."

"You needed shoes." He bent, and I could only stare in astonishment as he lifted each of my feet and put the shoes on. The sandals fit a bit large but were better than being barefoot.

"You stole shoes for me?" It was the cutest thing anyone had ever done for me.

Rather than reply, he stood and took my hand. "We should go in case someone heard that."

We walked quickly, following Murphy's suddenly moving butt, our pace rapid until we turned the next corner. The busier street had cars passing by.

"We need a cab," Urion declared, eyeing the traffic.

"Good luck finding one without a phone or a credit card." The days of them wandering streets aimlessly had ended with the riding apps.

"You make a compelling point." He began walking toward the corner with its light. I followed, mostly because I had no better place to go. Murphy kept pace.

"What are you planning?"

"You'll see."

Mysterious, not entirely reassuring, but what other option did I have?

The light turned red, and Urion stepped onto the road, but rather than cross, he moved to the driver's side of the car waiting for the green.

I could only gape as Urion dragged the driver out, the man pleading, "Take it. Don't hurt me."

"Get in," Urion barked, not apologizing for scaring the man who ran off soon as he could.

"You know he's going to call the cops," I said as I neared the hijacked car.

"Not quickly. I have his phone." He pointed inside where it sat in a cradle. "Get in."

I opened the backseat for Murphy, knowing we were probably being stared at by everyone who zoomed by. Urion hit the gas and sped off, handling the vehicle like a racecar driver. Speeding, taking corners tight and too fast.

We were in it a total of ten minutes before he pulled to a curb on a quiet, residential side street. He grabbed a multi tool found inside the console and got out. I gaped as he swapped the plates with another vehicle. He did it again a few blocks later. It was then I noticed he went after vehicles of the same model as our stolen one.

As we got on our way for the third and maybe final time I said, "You're good at this."

He spared me a glance. "Years of practice."

Would I become like him, willing to steal and maybe even harm to remain free?

He put his hand on my leg. I stared at it.

I might be willing to break all kinds of laws if I could be with him.

We drove around long enough that he had to stop for gas. Sitting in the passenger seat, I saw him go inside and talk with the attendant. He didn't rob him, which I took as a good sign.

When he got back into the driver's seat, he said, "I know where we need to go."

The instructions took us out of the newer parts of the city to the older section. The buildings got shabbier, bars blocked storefront windows. We'd found the wrong side of the tracks. Nervous, I locked my car door, and he chuckled.

"As if that will stop anyone."

He could laugh if he wanted, but I felt better, especially since despite the growing dereliction I saw signs of life. People pushing carts piled high with possessions. Fires set inside metal barrels, flames illuminating the faces gathered around and giving them a demonic cast.

The homeless of the city. The unlucky, unwanted, and forgotten. Would I become one of them?

Urion pulled over to where a few of the lit garbage cans clustered. As he exited the car, he tossed the keys to someone sitting on the ground, leaning against the brick wall, as if it held them up. The seemingly sleeping body caught the keys, and from under a knot of hanging hair, eyes gleamed yellow.

The uncanniness of it led to me stumbling as Urion tugged at my hand. Startled, I at least knew better than to remark on the oddity. I instead blurted out, "Why did you give him the keys? Aren't we going to need them?" How else would we leave?

"Given the cops will be looking, we need that car to disappear. Don't worry. I can get us another."

I had no doubt he could steal any car he wanted. Urion was a bad, bad boy. But did I run away?

Nope. I kept my fingers laced in his, partially because this place spooked me. It should be noted, as a woman, I'd long refused to use underground parking or walk alone outside at night.

Urion didn't seem bothered by the stares we drew. He probably didn't shiver or have the skin on his back prickling. I could only hope the darkness and the switch of my skirt hid any sign of my tail.

As we walked past a line of warehouses, some of them boarded, others chained shut, we encountered railroad tracks. Some were obviously still in use, the metal rubbed clean. Others had rusted and fallen into disrepair. According to my dad, during my history lessons, the manufacturing in many places across America had fled to foreign countries with laxer laws and cheaper labor.

For a while, there was hope it might come back. The pandemic had made it clear that the USA was vulnerable, but money and politics proved stronger than common sense. My dad used to rail about the fact we'd learned nothing. The country barely survived the economic disaster, and if it happened again, my father had predicted the end of America.

I missed my dad and his political rants.

Head ducked, I stumbled along with Urion and hadn't realized Murphy had gotten ahead until I heard him growling. I snapped to attention and saw my dog outlined by yet another barrel of fire. I might be wrong, but he seemed bigger than usual with all his fur bristling.

"Murphy," I called, but he appeared determined to stand his ground.

From the shadows, past the hellish glow of the barrel, a voice that sounded as if it had smoked too many cigarettes in its life exclaimed, "Doesn't he look tasty. Bet he'd make a nice roast."

"Don't you dare touch my dog," I said, moving close enough to put my hand on a bristling Murphy.

"Your dog. Ha. His kind aren't known to take orders very well. Especially the mixed breeds."

"Sorry we disturbed. We're leaving." Said more to my dog than the voice that wanted to eat him.

"Why don't you come close, child."

"I'm not a child," I declared and kept walking, only to find myself moving in the direction of the barrel. I tried to turn, but no matter what I did, I kept going toward the fire. Panicked, I huffed, "Urion, what's happening?"

Urion stepped close. "It's magic," he muttered.

Magic? I didn't exclaim my incredulity aloud. I couldn't exactly deny something weird was happening. I stopped abruptly, and no matter how I strained, my feet wouldn't move.

"I can't move," I whispered.

From the shadows, a hunched figure moved closer. My gut screamed in warning.

"Of course, you can't, because you and I need to discuss some business, Kalini." The robed figure could have been an alien for all I knew. I couldn't see a face or discern an expression or mood. It didn't help my anxiety levels.

"How do you know my name?" I asked, hoping she didn't hear the high pitch of anxiety in the query.

"I know a lot of things. Ask me a question."

"What's your name?" I asked. "Who are you?"

The figure uttered a noisy snort. "Why waste a question when he knows?"

"Urion?" My feet were planted, but my head could move. I turned to glance at him. "Do you know this person?"

"Unfortunately. Magda, the witch. What luck for me. I was hoping I'd find you. You and I have a score to settle." Urion bristled by my side.

"Why so angry?"

"As if you don't remember that stupid riddle you told me. When I asked you to explain it, you told me to have a few drinks at the Shaved Goat and all would come clear."

"Best lager ever." The moist smack of unseen lips brought a shudder.

"Because of you, I got captured and held prisoner by whitecoats," Urion snarled.

"Guess you should have paid attention to the riddle." Magda sounded unapologetic.

"Or you could have said, 'Dumbass, stay away from the fucking Shaved Goat' instead of sending me there."

"You asked me how to find happiness." The hunched figure walked away from the barrel of fire.

"Still waiting for it," Urion retorted as he followed. I stuck close. No way was I straying far from his side in this scary place.

"Never gave you a time frame," Magda declared. "You'll be glad to know you're getting close to it, though."

"What?" His jaw dropped, but before he could say more, Magda whirled and pointed a gnarled finger at me. "You. You should ask me about your tail." Stunning words spoken just as Magda entered a pitched tent.

I almost ran in after her.

*What about my tail?*

"What fucking bullshit!" he exclaimed.

I didn't disagree, but I did have questions. "You've met Magda before?"

"Yeah. The same day I was taken by the whitecoats." He scowled.

"Did she help them capture you?" Because he'd implied and she'd not exactly denied.

His jaw worked. "Yes. Why else tell me to go there?"

"You called her a witch. She does magic like making me go where I don't want to?"

"That's only the start. Magda is most known because she can foresee possible futures."

"Futures in the plural?"

"As if there's only ever one outcome. It always depends on choice." He grabbed my hand. "Let's go."

"Where?"

"To find help from someone other than this charlatan."

I glanced at the tent. I didn't say a word, and yet he sighed and said, "You want to ask her what she meant about your tail."

It had preyed on me from the moment she dropped it there, like a hot turd in the sun. The smell of it lingered, and I couldn't ignore it. It had to be dealt with, or it would fester. I had a dog. I knew this from experience. You couldn't be lazy with some things.

I turned my gaze on Urion. "Maybe she can see what's wrong with it."

"Or she'll lie. She will most definitely demand an outrageous price."

"What did she ask from you?"

"Something unlikely, and worthless. She knew I'd say yes and probably planned all along to turn me in to the whitecoats. They're the ones with the money."

"If she did it once, she could do it again." I glanced at the tent. Maybe we should be moving?

"You're right. This will torment you unless we find out more. So we'd better hurry and ask questions." Urion ducked into the tent first, with me right on his heels and Murphy on mine.

I doubted we'd all fit inside, yet as I entered, to my surprise, I noticed I could stand. As a matter of fact, it appeared more spacious than expected.

Magic.

Right in front of me.

Mind so utterly blown. Then curious.

If I'd expected strung bouquets of dried herbs, jars of floating grossness, or a cauldron, I was sorely disappointed. Magda didn't even have a crystal ball on display. What she did have was a plaid recliner, patched all over, and a basket beside it overflowing with yarn. The walls and roof of the tent were hidden in shadows. Anything could have been hiding in them.

Spooky.

Magda pulled her hood back and hung her cloak on a hook that just suddenly appeared.

I gasped.

Urion made a disdainful sound. "Parlor tricks."

"My parlor, which means mind your words, boy," Magda warned as she sat upon her tattered throne. The woman herself wasn't as old as I'd expected. Then again, age would be hard to determine with every inch of her tattooed. She also wore piercings in her nose, tongue, lips, ears. She'd shaved her head and her ears, pointed at the tip, bore a line of tiny gold hoops.

And she smelled... "Like black licorice." The flavor slipped from my lips.

Magda's lips quirked. "Anise is the proper name for it. And since you don't recognize what that means, I'll explain. I am a sorceress."

"Fancy name for a witch," Urion drawled.

"I wouldn't talk about names. I know what fathered you," Magda declared.

The claim dropped his head. How dare that woman make him feel bad? "If you can see things, then you know he had no choice in his parents. Neither of us did."

"No child ever does. And while it might not be fair, the sins of the parents are passed down to the next generation."

"You can shut your mouth about me. We only came inside to hear about Kalini's tail," was his gruff reminder.

"Are you sure that's what you want to ask me?" The witch's gaze pierced me. "I can see the future. The past. Maybe you're looking for the thing you want most."

"Don't fall for that trick," Urion interrupted.

"Soon, boy, you'll see just how right I was. And then I'll come for my due."

"As if I'll believe a word from your mouth," he snapped, and yet for some reason, he glanced at me.

What did it mean?

Magda smirked. "You'll be changing your tune soon enough and whining to renegotiate. The answer will be no by the way." Her gaze slewed to me. "But today is not about you, exiled one. It's about Kalini. Shall we negotiate?"

Suddenly it was as if a bubble went around me and the old lady. I could see Urion through it but barely, and he didn't move.

"What are you doing?" I exclaimed.

"Our deal is between us and us alone, girl. What do you want? Ask me your question."

"First, tell me the price."

She whispered it to me. "The shell of your first born."

I grimaced. "Gross."

"Will you pay?"

I nodded. It wasn't ever likely to come to pass. First off, I didn't lay eggs. I didn't have periods, either. I was sterile. "I'll pay."

"Pay what?" Urion asked as the privacy bubble vanished.

"None of your business," I snapped. "Tell me what's wrong with my tail." I expected Magda to touch my tail and geared myself for it.

Instead, she stared, and under her strange gaze, I squirmed. She muttered, "Let's see what's inside."

She apparently meant that quite literally. It felt as if Magda pried inside my mind, ghostly, sharp fingers tugging and poking. When that didn't yield everything she wanted, a spidery spirit wind tickled over my body and brought goosebumps to my flesh.

"What are you doing to her?" Urion asked as my breathing quickened.

"Something is wrong with the girl," Magda murmured. "Her essence is all knotted."

Could everyone see just how broken I was? "Thanks for reminding me I was created in a lab as part of an experiment." My words emerged bitten and tight.

"I'm not talking about your genetics, girl. I see a blockage inside you. An unnatural thing implanted in your flesh meant to keep you from accessing your full potential."

It sounded so specific and impossible, but I had to

wonder. Could my parents have meddled with me somehow?

"Are you talking about an implant?" I asked. "Impossible. I would have seen it."

"Even I can't see my ass without help," Urion declared, making me yearn to see said ass.

Magda doubled down. "There is something in you, girl. Something that doesn't belong. It should be removed. Strip and I will inspect you."

"Like hell you will," I quickly stated.

"Actually, that's not a bad idea." Urion switched sides.

I shot him a look of annoyance. "There's nothing there."

"Are you really one hundred percent certain?" he prodded.

I wanted to say yes. I'd have known if an alien object resided inside me. "I'll use mirrors."

"It doesn't have to be the witch." Urion grabbed my hands. "Let me look."

Let him see me in my full appendaged glory? I couldn't. What if he found it repugnant?

He dragged me close to murmur, "I know you want to say no, but think about it. What if this entire time you've had a physical reason you can't shift?"

I thought of something more horrifying. "What if there is nothing there and I truly am just a mistake?"

He whispered against my ear. "Never a mistake."

Magda cleared her throat. "I have other clients."

Urion glanced out of her tent. No one stood out front. "I can see they're waiting impatiently."

"Smartass. And you wonder why last time I gave you a riddle."

"That riddle put me in a coma for years."

Magda snorted. "It will all become clear soon. We're done and so are the pot brownies Beverly is making."

No, we weren't done. I had so many things I wanted to ask. "I have more questions."

"But you have nothing else that I want," was Magda's cackle as she swept out of the tent. The moment she left, the tent shrank.

"Let's get out of here." Urion dragged me out into the night=, and a barrel where the flames now burned low. Of Magda, I saw no sign, but Urion didn't appear to want to take any chances.

"Where are we going?" I said as he tugged me to follow. Murphy, who'd not come into the tent, trotted alongside.

"We are going somewhere far from here just in case she ratted us out."

I glanced over my shoulder. "You think she would?"

"I'm not taking the chance."

"Where are we going?"

He stopped suddenly and whirled. "I don't know." He raked a hand through his hair. "I came here hoping I'd find a dragon. Someone who could help you."

"You mean help us."

He ducked his head. "I can't be helped."

"I'm sure that's not true." On impulse I reached for him, putting my hand on his chest.

He shuddered. Long and hard. His gaze turned intent. Focused on me. "You wouldn't say that if you knew."

I suspected he'd done bad things to stay alive. Could I blame him? Not really. If forced to fight to survive... I'd like to think I'd rise to the challenge.

I leaned up and kissed him. I didn't ask. I didn't hesitate. And he groaned, kissing me back for a second before setting me aside. "Fucking me is not the answer to any of your problems."

My lips quirked. "Don't be so sure of that." I could almost guarantee sex with Urion would make me very happy.

Once more he trembled. His words emerged gruff. "Don't tempt me."

What if I wanted him tempted, though?

For a man who had no idea where he wanted to go, he followed a rather determined path. It led to us going up some stairs, after which he boosted me onto an old fire escape. Which, I'll admit, I kept expecting to plunge to the ground.

Murphy, my suddenly active and adventurous dog, made it to the top without help. Which made me wonder if he could be trained to not only put himself outside as needed but dispose of his business, too. Big dog meant super-sized poop. I had gagged more than once.

We climbed to the top floor, where a window gaped. He climbed in first before turning to offer me a hand. I clambered into an apartment long abandoned and yet used on occasion, judging by the garbage and the graffiti.

But we weren't staying in that room. He pulled me through a door that sat ajar, following Murphy's bushy tail.

The fire escape at the far end of the hall had its door propped open. We went up to the roof. A roof set up with an old couch, a few chairs, and a view.

Romantic until he said, without even a single kiss, "Take off your clothes.

## CHAPTER 19

DEAR DIARY: I FAILED BEING A SEXY SEDUCTRESS.

My reply? "You want me to get naked right now?"

"We really should check for a hidden device."

It hit me he wasn't asking me to remove my clothes for sexual reasons. How deflating. "I'd rather not."

"We have to know, Kalini." He placed his hands on my hips and gazed down at me. "It will be okay."

No, it wouldn't. Either my parents harmed me and lied some more or he'd realize this was as good as I got. I bit my lip and struggled to not cry.

He hugged me close. "It will be okay. I promise."

There was nothing logical about my decision to trust him. But I did. "Let's do this."

"Actually, let me," he said, putting his hand over mine when it gripped the waistband.

I trembled as he tugged my skirt down. The night air kissed my skin. Legs. The part of my ass not covered by tail.

There was something humiliating about standing

there while I was inspected. Dehumanizing. But it wasn't Urion's fault. He didn't do anything untoward. I didn't feel a thing as he examined my tail. He touched and saw everything.

I'd never felt more exposed.

And for nothing.

"I don't see or feel a thing," he admitted finally.

My shoulders slumped so far I probably regressed to BC evolution. "There's nothing there." Dejected, woe is me. Yeah. I'd finally hit that bottom.

He whirled me into his arms. "So what if there isn't? What we look like isn't what's in here." He pressed my hand to his chest. "This is what matters most."

I leaned my forehead onto his chest. "You make me want to believe that so badly."

He tilted my chin until I looked into his eyes. "Because it's true." Said a moment before his mouth claimed mine. He kissed me. Deeply. Slowly. Tugging each of my lips with languorous attention. Drawing my hitching breath into his mouth. Parting my lips for his tongue.

His hands cupped my ass cheeks, gripping me and rubbing me against him. His erection pressed against me, hard and thick. Wanting me despite seeing me with all my flaws.

I wanted him. Inside me. Now.

My hands went to his pants, and I undid them,

pushing them down low enough his cock sprang free. I grabbed him.

He hissed. His hips arched.

I smiled into his mouth. Whispered, "I want you."

He growled, like literally, and lifted me as he stalked over to one of the sturdier-looking plastic chairs. He sat on it and then put me in his lap. I turned and got awkwardly caught for a second, my leg bending enough my knee hit me in the chin. I saw stars but didn't fall to the floor as he held me and chuckled.

I recovered enough to squint at him. "Not funny."

He pulled me upright as my leg finally flopped to the other side of him. "You're right. Beautiful."

He kissed me, and the passion ignited fast and furious. I grabbed him and rubbed him on me, stroking the fat head of his dick against my clit. Moaning at the sensation.

His hands held me up as I moved to take him into me, pushing the thickness past the tight ring of pussy. I used my fingers to dig into his shoulders as I sat myself down and sighed in pleasure.

He filled me to perfection. I wiggled.

We both made an ungodly noise. So I did it again and again, rocking on him, driving him deeper and deeper. Oh, how I loved the feel of him throbbing inside.

As he grabbed hold of my hips and helped push and pull me, my pleasure built. My forehead leaned against his. Our breaths mingled. As I started to climax, my muscles tightened and he hissed, throwing his head back.

The smooth column of his neck beckoned, and I licked it.

He roared and bucked, his hips thrusting under me. I gasped, and my orgasm, still burgeoning, started over, stronger than before. My head tilted, and it was his turn for his mouth to graze me. To gently bite. I wasn't as nice. I bit the flesh between his neck and shoulder, imbued with an urge to chomp.

I might have done it a tad hard, because he cried out and tensed. I'd swear he came a second time, which made me come a third.

The force of it had me jerking and thrashing. Urion held me, and through a roaring in my ears, I heard him calling my name. I couldn't reply. A pressure inside me suddenly built. Expanding. Pushing.

It erupted from me in a blast of purple lightning that hit Urion. His eyes widened, but he didn't fry, as the electricity deflected back into me.

I screamed.

## CHAPTER 20

THE GENETIC MIXTURE IS MORE DEADLY THAN EXPECTED. IT IS RECOMMENDED TO TERMINATE SUBJECT Z.

Urion didn't know what to do as Kalini convulsed and screamed. He'd not known her capable of shooting lightning.

And she didn't know he was protected against it.

Now she paid the price, hit by her own power, but not burning. Thank fuck she wasn't burning, but why was her skin changing color?

It turned mauve, getting darker by the second, and the texture took on a scaly cast. It hit him that she was shifting in slow motion. Limbs popped out like balloons suddenly inflated.

*Boop.*

*Bop.*

*Bonk.*

Even her tail got a new look.

By the time it was done, a sleek purple dragon lay on the roof. She raised a groggy head crowned with a pair of metal horns, between which electricity zapped.

Cool.

Murphy appeared less than impressed and went back to sleep.

She sat up and eyed him, eyes drooping. She bugled something.

Did a double take. Blarted again and he laughed.

"You should see your face right now," he said, getting to his feet. "Or should I say muzzle? You're a dragon."

Her jaw worked, but nothing came out. She glanced down. Stood. Looked again. Held out her arms, which weren't T-Rex short like some illustrations showed. From her back projected the knobby peaks of her wings. They fluttered in agitation, which froze her. She glanced over her shoulder, and this time there was no mistaking a squeal.

He grinned. "Why don't you try and fly?"

She stared at him. He could almost see the cogs in her head turning. Then she cocked it and rolled her shoulders.

She didn't know how.

He did, but that would mean showing her his true self. Letting her in on his dangerous secret.

The last person he let close enough to show had betrayed him.

Would it be different with Kalini? He'd known her barely a few days. Intense days. He recognized her on a different level. Wanted her like nothing he'd ever imagined.

Would do anything for her.

Except show her his dark side.

"It's easy. Flap your wings." He bounced his arms.

She huffed and bounced, fluttering them.

He laughed. "Don't be afraid to open them up. Spread those wings and fly."

She lifted them, and they snapped to full length. A pale mauve veined in darker mauve with some gold.

Beautiful. Unlike him.

She waddled to the side of the building and looked down. Glanced at him as if to ask permission.

He shrugged. "You'll heal eventually if you miss."

She squawked and might have taken forever to decide if they'd not suddenly had company, and him with his pants still undone. Great. Just fucking great.

He yanked and tucked as he whirled to see who disturbed them.

Too slow as it turned out. A rifle emerged first and fired. Kalini squealed, and as he watched, she lost her footing and fell off the roof.

That was when he lost his shit.

"Grawr."

He transformed into his dark half, which led to wild shots that stung. Tranquilizers that tried to sedate. With the immunity he'd built up, they'd need a much larger dose. They'd be dead before that happened.

"Dinner time." His words had a guttural and gruff sound to them that widened the eyes on the humans hunting him. They raised their weapons to strike, knowing they'd have at least one shot before he could reach them on foot. They didn't count on Murphy taking out one of the shooters. The big dog did a silent pounce. Not that Urion needed the help.

Apparently, no one told the retrieval squad he didn't need to touch them to grab their minds.

Their screams were music. Their abrupt cessation a sign he'd taken control. In mere seconds, the soldiers sent by the whitecoats had turned their weapons on each other.

He ran for the edge of the roof in time to see Kalini fly.

## CHAPTER 21

DEAR DIARY: I HAD EPIC SEX. OH, AND I'M A DRAGON.

Yes, a dragon, who was falling awfully fast.

My mouth opened in a bugling honk of noise as I spread my arms, which happened to spread my wings.

*Snap.*

The air caught them and jolted me hard enough I careened into a building, bounced off, and was heading for the ground again when instinct chipped in. I banked. Or turned. Did fucking something that had me soaring again. Apparently I didn't need to concentrate too hard for my wings to know what to do.

Cool.

So cool, I had forgotten why I fell off the building in the first place.

The screams drew me back. I flew—yes flew, goddammit—back to the roof where I'd left Urion. Only Urion was gone, and in his place was a big beast.

And I mean big. Kind of like a dragon crossed with evil. Spikes up and down his spine between the wings.

Spurs on his heels. Clawed hands. But I soon realized he didn't have to touch to hurt.

The humans moaned and yelled. A few held their heads. They were the first to go when the wild-eyed ones started shooting.

It didn't take long for the big bad dragon and my dog to be the only living things on that roof. And for me to realize who it was.

I landed beside Urion. Skidded. Went a few steps. Stopped again and whirled. I wondered if I'd made a mistake when I noticed Hell shone in his eyes. A red fire that glowed in his irises and even rose in the tracings running over his body. Not tattoos or birthmarks but scars.

So many scars. My poor Urion.

On instinct alone, I switched shapes—less painful than my initial transformation, thank fuck. He saw me and huffed. Burnt nutmeg over scorched milk. Still delicious to me. Naked, and not caring, I walked over to Urion and stood before him.

Eyes glowing with Hades fire could still show confusion and shame. He ducked his head, tried to turn away. Shrank into his other self. No scars on that body. I wondered what it meant.

"Are you okay?" he asked, worried about me.

I couldn't help a cocky grin. "I'm a dragon. So hell yeah I'm okay."

He returned my smile. "And a gorgeous dragon at that."

"Guess it's a good thing I like purple." Even if it clashed with my yellow outfits. "My tail is gone."

"You broke through whatever barrier blocked you from shifting."

Speaking of which. "The morphing thing is hard on clothes."

He chuckled. "You learn to carry spares."

I threw my arms around him. "Thank you."

"For what?"

"Coming into my life. Making me whole. Happy."

He froze. Then withdrew enough to stare at me intently. "And I've never been happier than when I'm with you," he said, and then groaned. "That witch."

"Does that mean you owe her an apology?"

"Fuck no, because guess who probably sent those guys after us." He swept a hand at the bodies.

"Hey, since I'm a dragon now, does that mean I can eat her?"

"Only if you want indigestion. Besides, her plan didn't work."

I smiled. "No, it didn't." And now the future was rosy. "Can we go find somewhere a little less bloody and maybe locate some underpants? Feeling a little exposed." My girly parts definitely felt a breeze.

"If we fly back downtown, we can probably hit a condo with a balcony. They never lock their sliding glass doors."

"Already making me into a thief."

"I'll get a job if you want me to." He sounded pained even suggesting it.

"Earning an honest paycheck won't kill you."

"Your last job would have."

"So we work in the food industry instead of the medical field."

"I am not slinging burgers."

As we moved to the edge of the roof, I paused. Did I hear something?

I had only a second to whirl, just enough time to see the second wave of humans pouring onto the roof, guns aimed to fire. There was no way they would have missed. I was taking in a breath, wondering if I'd have time to shift, when a sheet of fire fell from the sky, intense enough that no one screamed.

I had no breath to squeak as a dragon landed on the roof. A giant beast with dark, rusty scales, who eyed me. It bugled, and despite not hearing words, I understood what it wanted. I shifted.

The dragon before me uttered a sound, and then there was a woman standing there, crying.

"My daughter. At last I've found you."

## CHAPTER 22

DEAR DIARY: I'M NOT AN ORPHAN ANYMORE.

THAT QUICKLY I slipped back into my human skin. "You're my mother?" It had never occurred to me that the one who'd laid my egg might still be around. "How can you be sure?"

"Because blood knows blood." She sounded so firm. "They might have stolen you from my nest, but I always hoped one day I'd find you."

"Listen to her, Kalini," Urion encouraged.

Red Dragon—*my mom?*—hissed. "Stay back, foul thing."

"Don't call him that. His name is Urion. He's a dragon like us." Mostly. He obviously had some other parts, too.

"He's an abomination," new mom insisted.

My chin lifted. "So am I then since I was also messed with in a lab."

"You don't carry the wicked genetics he does."

This family reunion sank more quickly than the

*Titanic.* "Don't talk about Urion like that. I don't care if you don't like what his genetic cocktail consists of. The man himself is awesome."

"He's a demon."

"Part demon," Urion corrected.

"So what?" I burst out. "That doesn't make him evil."

"Perhaps not, but it does mean he's forbidden from entering Limbo. Given the issues demons cause, they're not allowed inside."

"Limbo exists?" Urion asked. "Can Kalini find safety there?"

"She can." The implication was clear.

Like hell. "I'm not going if you're not allowed," I hastened to say.

He shook his head. "You're going. It's the only way you'll be safe."

"You should listen to the demi-demon. He's actually talking sensibly."

I glared at my newfound egg donor. "Don't talk about Urion like that. He's a good man. They can make an exception."

"To argue his case, you'll have to come with me." My new mom lifted her chin with triumph. Hard to pull off snooty when naked, but she did it.

I will admit it was super weird to me that my lover was seeing her naked while he was naked and I was naked. Holy nakedness all around.

My world had tilted upside down. It moved too quickly. "I need time to think."

"No, you don't." Urion came closer, and egg-mom growled. "Let me talk to Kalini for a minute. Then you can take her."

"You have sixty seconds. Then I roast you."

Egg-mom moved off to sniff at the bodies, and Urion grabbed my hands. "I don't have much time other than to say you need to go. This is your chance to live without hiding. To be with family who can teach you where you come from."

"Not without you."

"You heard what she said. I'm not allowed in."

"Then I'll talk to whoever made the rule."

"Do that." He acquiesced too easily.

It hit me hard. "You think once I get there, I won't come back."

He shrugged. "You don't owe me anything."

"I owe you my life." I hissed.

"And I'm giving it back to you. Use this chance, Kalini. Be happy. For the both of us." He kissed me hard.

A goodbye kiss before he launched himself from me, snapping into his demon/dragon misfit shape. Leaving me.

Because he thought it was best.

*I'll decide what's best for me.*

New mom returned to my side. "At least he didn't argue. Shall we?"

"I don't even know your name." The wrong thing to say given the pang that hit the woman's face.

"I'm Heidi."

"And my dad?"

Her lips pursed. "Having seen your colors, it obviously wasn't who I thought it was."

I blinked at her.

"It was the winter solstice. I had a lot to drink. He's going to be a tad surprised when he finds out you exist."

"So I wasn't made in a lab?" I asked.

"Not entirely. But you were changed. The horns are interesting. And purple..." Her lips pursed. "That will set the hierarchy abuzz. There hasn't been a new color in...ever, actually."

Leave it to me to still be different.

"Is Limbo truly a safe place for someone like me?"

"Yes."

"And my dog?"

"Yes. Yes. Now come here and hug me." My mother, Heidi, still naked, tried to give me a squeeze.

I shied away. "Personal space, lady, until we have some clothes."

"Prudish like a human. We'll have to teach you the right ways. Shall we go home?" She shifted, and after a second of looking at the sky, wondering if Urion would come back, I changed into my dragon, too, and with my dog racing along below us on the ground, within the hour, I was in a whole new world. But I didn't forget my promise.

---

*How long before she forgets me?*

Urion trailed at a distance, ensuring Kalini arrived at their destination safely. The portal to Limbo was hidden in the basement of a tattoo parlor. Long after she left, he presented himself in the off chance the elder dragon had lied.

The mocking derision, uttered by the guardian of the gate, followed him as he flew as far away as he could.

## CHAPTER 23

DEAR DIARY: SINEAD O'CONNOR SANG IT
BEST IN THAT HIT SONG OF HERS.

I missed Urion something fierce.

Even if my mom didn't think I should.

At first glance, and even second, Limbo appeared a paradise. From the moment we entered the gate I felt the difference.

First off, I should mention the fellow granting passage looked an awful lot like that bad pirate with the tentacles on his head in that movie with the chameleon actor, Johnny Depp. He spoke perfect, clipped English and smelled of lilacs of all things.

The arch itself was made of two-by-fours nailed together and pressed against a basement wall. Only when I had permission from Tentacle Guardian did it swirl into a scary fucking portal. Like a black hole that oozed bone-chilling cold.

I'll admit, I balked. I dug my fingers into Murphy's fur.

What would I be stepping into?

As it turned out, Mommy was the impatient sort and she shoved me through. I emerged, stumbling onto flagstones placed to appear like a flower with the arch in the middle. Around the petals of stone stretched a verdant park sporting vibrant grass. Looping through the field of green were paths being used by misfits like me.

Some had human bodies, wearing all manner of clothing. But the centaur chose to hang loose, as did the yeti with hair all over except for its face and ass.

I stood and stared long enough that my mother snapped her fingers. "You shouldn't stare."

"I'm just surprised to see so much nudity. Don't people care?"

"Care about what? Humans can be such prudes," my new mom scoffed.

"How come there's no guard on this side?" I asked.

"This isn't a prison. And besides, who leaves paradise?"

I quickly understand what she meant. Not only was the place gorgeous, I could be myself here. Overhead, there were those who flew, the sizes and colors changing. Some avian. Some dragon. Some things I'd never imagined. On the ground, I saw fur and horns, even a fabled unicorn. As my mother led me past a fountain, a glimpse within showed toddler mermaids cavorting.

"Oh, how adorable."

"Don't put your hand in there. They'll strip it to

bone," my mother warned.

I skirted the edge and after that realized not everyone was cute and cuddly. I noticed the really big teeth. Scary faces. Massive claws capable of cutting me in half.

"Does everyone get along?" I asked as we passed a woman wearing snakes on her head.

"While a little bit of steam-letting is expected, cross a certain line and the queen will come down hard on you."

"Queen?"

"She likes people to call her Beth. She rules with her consorts, Simon and Gene."

This led to Heidi launching into a brief history lesson, brief because Limbo had, until recently, been under a curse. Then Beth, a misfit of angel and demon, gave her life to stop a curse and *boom*! Misfitia was born. Apparently, a book was written about it, titled *Hybrid Misfit,* available in e-book, paperback, and audio.

"Hold on a second," I said. "You just said Beth is part demon. How come she's allowed to be here but Urion isn't?"

"Because she freed Limbo."

"That seems unfair."

And my egg mother couldn't change my mind on that. Which was why, despite the allure of Limbo, I pestered and petitioned until I got to speak with the queen.

## CHAPTER 24

SUBJECT Z REPEATEDLY IGNORES OUR WARNINGS AND CONTINUES TO BEFRIEND OTHERS. GIVEN SUBJECT R'S USELESSNESS, WE'VE CHOSEN TO TERMINATE HIM TO MAKE AN EXAMPLE AND PROVIDE A BODY FOR STUDY.

URION THOUGHT HE KNEW LONELINESS. After all, his life had consisted of it. But the crushing ache that hit him when Kalini left had no compare.

What was the point? Why did he keep trying? It was clear he didn't fit in anywhere. Not on Earth or Limbo. Would he even be considered demonic enough for Hell?

*I am not going to Hell.*

Perhaps it would be easier to let the whitecoats catch him and put him back to sleep.

Or maybe it was time to fulfill the destiny that had gotten him locked up in the first place? As a teen, he'd convinced the doctors that he had the ability to destroy the world. That belief persisted even once he left, their terror taking on a life of its own. Scare one person well enough and then they actually scare the next for you. And the next. The problem being fear led to fatal outcomes.

Saw him hunted.

Could he destroy the world? Maybe if he got into the mind of the right person with access to nukes. But it wouldn't make him feel better.

He missed Kalini.

And as if that were a wish, he heard her voice. "Urion."

He crouched like a gargoyle upon a building chosen for its height—and the pizza on the first floor. If he dropped down quick enough, he could get the ones they tossed in the dumpster before the rats or the homeless did. Although he didn't keep the ones with pineapple. That was just wrong.

"Urion, I know you can hear me."

He crouched lower. It couldn't be her. She couldn't have found him. He'd flown for days. It had to be a trick.

"I told you I'd come back."

He honestly hadn't thought she would. He whirled but didn't change to his man shape. This was who he was. The monster everyone feared. The demon in him meant his dragon scales emerged black and dull, sucking in the light around them. His wings were massive and leathery. His claws sharp. His teeth sharper. Most dragons were elemental based. Fire. Ice. In Kalini's case, she had an unheard-of electrical ability.

For Urion, his magic was based in fear. In exploiting a person's innermost terror. Not only could he provoke it, he fed on it. Grew strong it. He should be feared. He'd done terrible things.

He muttered a gruff, "Go away, Kalini." She deserved better than him.

"I'm not going anywhere without you."

"Not interested, so you might as well hightail it back to Limbo." Please let her leave before he caved to his weakness. Before he ruined her chance at happiness.

"Do you miss me?" Before he could answer, she said, "I missed you. Ask me how I found you."

He didn't need to because he'd once used that same link to find her. They were bound. "We can't be together."

"Tell me you don't want me."

He pressed his lips. He should lie. He should be strong enough to do what was best for her. "Go." He whispered the word.

"No."

"Please, Kalini." He closed his eyes. "Don't you understand? I need you to be safe."

"Why do you get to decide what I need?"

"Because I love you!" he yelled, opening his eyes to stare at her with the passion that simmered inside him. "I love you, and I won't see you come to harm for me. I don't deserve it."

She cupped his cheeks. "And what makes you think you can be a martyr? Love doesn't sacrifice. It works together. Fights together. Stays together. You don't belong here. You belong with me in Limbo, which is why I spoke to the folks in charge."

"You did what?"

Her lips quirked. "I petitioned for them to let you in."

"Why would you fight for me?" In that moment, he had no arrogance. No hope.

She grabbed his hands and lifted on tiptoe to whisper on his lips. "Because you're the one I want. The one I love. The one I need more than anything."

It was the most amazing thing he'd ever heard.

So why did he hit the ground on his knees in front of her? Head bowed. Shaking.

She knelt and wrapped her arms around him. "Oh, Urion, I'm sorry I left you. I wish I'd had another way of fighting for you."

He kept shaking. She didn't understand. "You came back."

"I always will. I love you. Together forever, which I'm told might be a long time for us, if you'll have me."

As if she had to ask. Before he could reply, he heard it, the whirring of a chopper. The hiding, the running, would it never end?

"Come on, we have to go." This time she grabbed him by the hand.

"Go where?"

She pointed. "I got Jacques to open a doorway to Limbo not far from here."

"Jacques?" He bristled.

She laughed. "Don't be jealous. He's like a zillion years old, and I'm pretty sure he's related to Mr. Toad."

"What if I can't cross with you?"

She leaned in to kiss him and whisper, "Your turn to trust me."

It scared him, but the agony at losing her terrified him more. They leapt from the roof and transformed before the lights swept the surface. They coasted past the searching metal birds and soon dropped down into a plaza created as an oasis within the city, with deep benches spaced far apart, most only big enough for one person to sit.

They alighted, and she led him by hand to a sculpture, a man-made, waist-high stone hedge. As they neared, two of its monoliths grew. As they expanded, the guardian appeared. Not the one who'd laughed at him before. Jacques was a hulking beast of a man, twice the size, muscled, but green with a frog's head and giant eyes that perused him. He flicked his super-long pronged tongue.

"Your never told me he was demon. He can't pass," Jacques hissed.

"I have documentation that says otherwise." Kalini held up a scroll of paper tied in a golden ribbon. Unrolling it, he expected some legal treatise.

Instead he saw only a few bold and flourished words.

*Let Urion pass.* And a set of lips pressed into a golden seal.

It was enough for Jacques, who stepped aside and said, "Welcome to Limbo. Don't fuck it up."

"I don't plan to," he muttered, pausing by the arch.

Kalini whispered, "It will be okay."

He wanted to believe.

He trusted in her and stepped through the portal.

Emerging, he froze. The place seemed too perfect. Too bright.

Overhead, something with jewel-toned wings flew past in a strange sky, no sun, no clouds, only a wispy, illuminated, swirling mist. While he stood on a stone dais, verdant grass stretched with meandering paths, but it was the big bold sign overhead that had him blinking.

*Welcome to Misfitia.* And in smaller letters underneath was scrawled: *Only one rule, don't be a douchecanoe.*

## CHAPTER 25

DEAR DIARY: THIS MIGHT BE MY LAST ENTRY FOR A WHILE. I'M PLANNING TO SPEND A LOT MORE TIME IN BED.

POOR URION. The shock on his face. A good thing he didn't have to talk to anyone today. His meeting with the queen was first thing in the morning. By then maybe he'd relax.

I planned to help him with that relaxing. And tensing. And relaxing...

In the days it took me to get permission to bring Urion into Limbo and then locate him, I learned some of the Misfitia secrets. Such as how to move fast. To show him, I dragged him by the hand, each stride moving us more like ten. A strange magic that imbued the roads to avoid the use of vehicles.

In no time at all, we were at the cottage I'd been given. Everyone who arrived got a place, although its size and shit depended. Limbo had this thing about giving people what they needed and not necessarily what they wanted.

Apparently, I needed a super cute beachy cottage with a plunge pool in the back. I wasn't about to argue.

Urion stood staring at my place. Then left and right, as if waiting to be attacked.

"You're safe," I promised. It would take time for him to heal. To trust.

Holding his hand, I dragged him into the house. Our house.

Only he hesitated at the threshold. "Maybe I shouldn't."

I arched a brow. "What? Suddenly get to Limbo and now that you've got your choice of babes, I'm no longer good enough?"

His jaw dropped. "Are you out of your fucking mind? It's more like I'm not good enough for you. You're the only one I want."

"Then prove it," I dared. I pulled off my shirt and the bra I just couldn't ditch. My hands went to my skirt. Funny thing, it turned out I preferred wearing them to pants. Only now, I could go shorter.

I shimmied, and it hit the floor. My panties followed. There was something powerful and erotic about how he watched me.

I rolled my hips as I took the few steps needed to close the gap between us.

This time when he dropped to his knees, it was to worship me.

His tongue found me and stroked so well, so fast that I was crying out and thrusting my hips against his face. I was glad he had some wits about him because he caught me when my legs buckled. Carried me to the bedroom and tossed me on the bed.

He stripped and joined me, his body hot and heavy against mine.

We kissed. We licked. Our hands skimmed every inch. When he went all sixty-nine on me, I was ready to suck him, as he sucked me. We both came and then came again, as he slid into me, still hard, and as he stroked me, got harder. He took me from behind, one hand squeezing my breast, his dick buried in me, his other hand between my legs.

Stroking.

Thrusting.

Whispering in my ear, "I love you. Fuck, I love you."

And I screamed it, "Urion, I love you." Now and forever.

We collapsed in a heaving pile of sweaty, sated bliss. Fell asleep spooned.

Happy.

When I woke with a cramp, my hand grabbed for my lower belly and I wondered what was wrong with me.

"You okay?" My lover nuzzled against me.

"Tummy ache."

"Is it your cycle time?"

"Ew. No. I don't have periods. Ever. I don't have a uterus." When by sixteen I'd yet to have a period, my parents rented an ultrasound machine. That was when they found out. I'd been told it was part of my being special.

"Dragons don't have a uterus far as I know. They lay eggs," Urion stated.

"I know that." Actually, I didn't know much. I'd always assumed I was sterile. Couldn't have a baby without a uterus, after all. Although I did apparently possess one oversized ovary.

The pain continued, and rolling out of bed, I ignored Urion as I ran for the bathroom. Even in limbo, number ones and number twos still happened. I sat on that porcelain seat, cold on my butt, and felt an incredible pressure.

A knock at the door was followed by, "Kalini, are you okay?"

"Go away," I groaned. Because having cramps was not my idea of sexy morning after.

"What's wrong? Do you need a doctor?"

"No. I'm fine." A false statement finished on a high gasp as a terrible pain ripped through me, and then pressure. So much pressure. I bore down, wondering if I had to poop.

*Plop. Splash.*

Whatever fell in the toilet didn't come out of my butt, which led to me spreading my legs to look down.

Bobbing in the water was an egg.

"Oh my god."

"That's it. I'm coming in." The door was kicked open just as I plucked the egg from the toilet.

"I swear, this has never happened before," I squeaked.

As to what it meant? We took the egg to my mom's place, and she was the one to announce, "I'm going to be grandma."

A good thing my mom was quick. She saved the egg when Urion and I fainted.

**EPILOGUE**

Love proved wonderful and terrifying. Or so Urion discovered. It wasn't just astonishing that someone like Kalini could love him. It was the fact someone could mean so much.

And now that love was about to grow.

The egg had gotten too big to sit in the padded pouch Urion used to wear slung around his body. Given what had happened to them both, even though safe in Limbo, they couldn't help but guard it. The day came, though, when the egg grew to be too large for carrying, and his new mother-in-law smacked him and said he'd scramble the child if he didn't let it sit for a while. Despite his trepidation, at Kalini's urging, they sat eggy junior in a nest of blankets placed inside a basket that enjoyed the radiating heat from their potbelly stove, a heat source that appeared the day the egg outgrew the satchel. It never went out. It eased his mind that Murphy had taken to guarding the egg when he couldn't. Curling his big furry body around it.

According to his MIL—because hell yeah, he'd married his Kalini—the egg would hatch any day now.

Months of waiting almost over. Months of him adjusting to what it meant to not hide. Days and weeks of learning he could have a life. He even got a job! The queen herself hired him, which surprised him because, when the command arrived that he should present himself the morning after his arrival, he'd assumed the worst. Readied himself for the possibility they'd declare his admission a mistake and kill him. At the very least tell him he was undeserving and kick him out.

Kalini tried to reassure him. "You belong here with the rest of us misfits."

He wanted to believe, but it was hard even with Kalini's hand holding his as he stood at the foot of a dais with a throne made of clouds. Sitting upon it, an unexpected queen wearing a mini skirt and crop top, legs hanging over the side. Flanking the throne, a massive dude that he knew to be the ice dragon consort, Simon, and the wise and deadly djinn, Gene.

"Your Majesty." He inclined his head because he knelt for no one.

Queen Beth met his eyes and cocked her head. "Hello, Urion. Sorry we didn't get to meet yesterday when you arrived. Apparently ruling a kingdom doesn't mean eating cake all the time."

Was this an ass-kissing session? He could kiss ass if needed. "Thank you for allowing me to come despite your demon rule."

"You're not a full demon, thank fuck. They're usually sadistic assholes. And as for half ones, you're the only one aside from me that isn't a murdering vampire. Besides, I've always wanted an older brother."

He blinked at her and wanted to speak, just couldn't. The queen stepped off her throne and came down the steps. As she neared, he could smell her.

So did Kalini, and she said it first. "Queen Beth smells a lot like you."

"Because we're related. We have the same demonic father." The queen, his sister, reached for him, and he didn't realize he was crying until she hugged him and said, "It's okay. You're with family now. And no one hurts those I love."

The funny thing was he would die for those he loved, too. In one fell swoop, he had not only Kalini and an egg but he'd found a sister and two nephews, rowdy toddlers who had a tendency of climbing him to smother him in slobbery kisses. He found a home. A place to belong.

And all anyone demanded from him was love. Months later and he still couldn't believe it.

"Urion!" Kalini leaned over the basket and glanced at him over her shoulder, excitement shining in her eyes.

"Yes, my love." But he didn't need her to tell him it was time.

He sat cross-legged beside the basket and tugged his mate onto his lap. She nestled the egg in hers, and together they watched the crack that widened.

He'd been told, despite the urge to help, to let the fledgling break out on its own. They'd also been warned to expect the unexpected. Two misfits making a baby?

He'd love the child no matter what.

The cracks on the shell multiplied as it got hammered with blows. Finally, a chunk broke free. A fist poked through.

Chubby fingers covered in slightly tanned flesh. It retreated, and it wasn't just Kalini holding her breath.

With a mighty shove, their child rammed its head through the shell and popped into view, blinking the biggest purple eyes. Which were light in comparison to its mauve tuft of hair.

The baby, their baby, opened its mouth and cooed. It reached for Kalini, and she swept their—hold on, no outdoor plumbing down below—daughter into her arms.

Crying. Laughing. Hugging.

His daughter snuggled for a moment before raising her head to stare at him, and she gave him the biggest smile.

Her wings fluttered, and it was his turn for a hug. Loved already. She'd never know what it was like to fear being herself. She'd be raised among misfits, and they were all about to live their best life.

His happiness was complete.

Which meant Magda came for her due.

They handed over the broken shell. Every last piece. It seemed Magda wanted to hedge her bets when it came to acquiring it. And here he'd thought her nuts when she requested it long ago.

"What are you going to do with it?" Kalini asked.

"Stew."

Ew. Or is Magda lying? What about the whitecoats? We know they're still watching. Plotting. And are there still misfits alone and hiding in the world? Maybe I'll come across another one with a story to tell.

*For news and More books visit EveLanglais.com*

**Want more stories about experiments gone wrong?**

www.ingramcontent.com/pod-product-compliance
Lightning Source LLC
LaVergne TN
LVHW041635060526
838200LV00040B/1579